*S*himmer studied the stars overhead and then altered her course slightly. "That Widow is really a wicked creature called Civet. She stole my sea and put it into a blue pebble."

The cold wind blowing by my face was beginning to make my nose itch. "I've heard a tale about a witch doing that." I had only meant to show that I wasn't completely ignorant; but it was the wrong thing to say.

We dropped several meters through the air as Shimmer missed a beat of her wings. "It's a fine thing," she spluttered indignantly, "when the tragic history of your clan is reduced to a mere legend. You humans lead such short lives that the facts of one generation become the stories of the later ones. And for your information, she isn't a witch but the wife of a river spirit. She destroyed him some time ago and took over his spells and such. But though she made some trouble for our friends at River Glen, we really didn't worry about her. And then she came one night and took away our sea."

ALSO BY LAURENCE YEP

LAURENCE YEP

DRAGON OF THE LOST SEA

A Charlotte Zolotow Book

HarperTrophy
A Division of HarperCollinsPublishers

Library of Congress Cataloging-in-Publication Data
Yep, Laurence.
  Dragon of the lost sea.

  "A Charlotte Zolotow book."
  "A Harper Trophy book."
  Summary: Shimmer, a renegade dragon princess,
tries to redeem herself by capturing a witch with
the help of a human boy.
  I. Fantasy.   I. Title.
PZ7.Y44Dq 1982   [Fic]   81-48644
ISBN 0-06-026746-1   AACR2
ISBN 0-06-026747-X (lib. bdg.)
ISBN 0-06-440227-4 (pbk.)

First Harper Trophy edition, 1988.

A Scott Foresman Edition
ISBN 0-673-80139-X

To my grandmother,
Marie Lee

Dragon
of the
Lost Sea

CHAPTER ONE

I stopped when I smelled the magic. It was strong magic. Old magic. And it carried a faint scent of the sea. And yet I was a thousand kilometers away from the nearest body of salt water.

Halting in the middle of the road, I tried to follow the scent. It came from the top of a nearby hill, where a little village sat like a tray of dirty, overturned cups that someone had left to gather dust. But the magic I smelled was too powerful for a small, sleepy place like that.

Well, when trouble isn't drawn to me, I seem to be drawn to it. Leaning on my staff, I stepped off the main road onto the side path that wound through the rice fields.

One of the farmers looked up from his weeding. He stared at my bare, callused feet and then at my dirty, ragged blouse and finally at my old woman's wrinkled face. Almost immediately he made a sign against evil. I suppose he didn't want me infecting him with my poverty. "We don't allow beggars in Amity," he snapped.

Despite all the centuries I have spent disguised as a human, it never fails to amaze me how hard and flinty human hearts always are—though humans have such short lives that I suppose they have to eat and grasp as much as they can. "I'm not a beggar," I corrected him proudly. "I always earn my food."

"That's what they all say." He picked up a clod of dirt as if to throw it at me. "And then they steal whatever they can lay their hands on."

"Times are hard." I chose my words with care. "I didn't always look and dress like this." With as much dignity as I could, I tried to hobble on past him.

I was mistaken, though, if I thought I could shame him into leaving me alone. His clod of dirt hit me right in the middle of my back. "We don't want your kind here," he insisted.

I straightened slowly. *My kind* indeed. I daresay he'd be singing a far different tune if he knew I wasn't a human at all. I felt like turning around to teach that stupid farmer some manners when I suddenly caught another whiff of magic. It smelled not only of salt water but of *stagnant* salt water.

Even more curious now, I decided that I could always deal with the farmer later on. It was more important to investigate this odd bit of magic. So I forced myself to slouch once again like an old woman and trudged on past the rice fields and through the orchards of trees that clustered on the slopes of the hill until I reached the village gates.

The guard there wasn't any friendlier than the farmer below. "Keep out, old woman." He pointed his spear at me.

I squinted at him because he looked very much like the farmer who had thrown the clod of dirt at me. I always have a hard time telling humans apart— they have almost no features at all: such tiny eyes and such little snouts. And this one had the same brown hair and blue eyes as the farmer. "I'm willing to work," I told him.

"The times are so bad we barely manage to take care of our own." He jabbed at me halfheartedly with his spear. "You'd be better off trying your luck at some other village."

"But people always say the same thing at every place I go," I said—which was the truth. "And I've come such a long way and my belly aches so." I rubbed my stomach for emphasis. "Haven't you ever known what it is to be hungry?"

The guard looked away from me and wiped the back of his hand across his mouth. "Yes, I have." He raised his spear. "All right. You can try your luck; but I can tell you right now that you won't find anything."

I forced myself to smile and bow my head gratefully. (Of all the things I have had to learn how to do among humans, I think bowing my head has been the hardest—especially when the favor done for me is no favor at all.)

But once I was through the gates, I stopped almost immediately. There, sitting within the yard of an inn, was a wooden sedan chair, and squatting around the chair were four creatures who looked like men. And on the left side of the inn's doorway was a guard in a padded cotton coat. He held a huge cutlass in his hand. And all of them—the chair, the porters and the guard—reeked of the magic that had created them.

But who was their creator? This far inland, I could only think of one creature whose magic would smell like a stagnant sea, and that would be Civet, the great enemy of my clan.

Thief was too small a word for the size of her theft. Killer was too kind a word for the suffering she had brought to my clan. She was a wicked, cruel creature who seemed to delight in hurting others. She had come in the dead of night and stolen the entire sea of my clan, encapsulating it into an object the size of a pebble.

Of course, I had been away at the time, but the tales had spread throughout the land. So I had heard how she had retreated inside the Weeping Mountain. My clan pursued her as soon as it had recovered from its surprise; but they found that she had filled the mountain with all sorts of traps, soldiers and monsters. Very few who entered ever returned. Without the sea to shelter them, the survivors of my clan had been exposed to the cold and the terrible winds; and since they now had no way of getting food, they had been forced to abandon our ancient home and become wanderers and beggars within the other kingdoms.

Occasionally, in the following years, I had heard some tragic tale of one who had tired of that homeless life and tried to enter the Weeping Mountain to take our revenge and perhaps restore our home. But as yet no one had ever succeeded.

I could not understand what errand could draw Civet from her mountain; but it was an opportunity not to be missed. My luck had been so universally bad for all these centuries that at first it was hard to believe it was finally beginning to turn.

My heart began to pound and my pulse began to race. If I could just capture her and the pebble, I could end the long years of wandering for both myself and my clan. We could hold our heads proudly once again. And my clan would have to thank me for it all. They would probably be making up plays and songs for ten generations about my deeds.

My fingers arched involuntarily like claws. I would have liked nothing more than to change myself and charge inside; but the inn was too tiny for my true shape. And sneaking in there while I was disguised smacked of *her* kind of tactics. No, I would meet her out in the open in my true form.

But I had spent so much time that the guard began to look at me suspiciously. There was no sense making trouble until it was time. Quickly I showed him the palm of one hand and looked at him as if pleading for some cash. He chopped at the air disgustedly. I made a point of tottering on.

CHAPTER TWO

The houses of the village were really little more than muddy shacks, and yet each had its own wall and small courtyard. From past experience I knew that there, inside the yard, would be children or the family pig or trays of vegetables drying—or sometimes all three, the children trying to keep the pigs away from whatever food was there.

I had planned to sit by the village well, where someone was bound to be gossiping about the traveler staying at the inn. But when I got there, I found the villagers busy with other things.

There was a boy, about thirteen in human years, who wore a shirt and trousers more dirty and ragged than mine (which I would have said was impossible before I actually saw him). He was doing his best to draw a bucket of water from the well, while a group of boys and girls stood around taunting him.

"Thorn, tell us again about the Unicorn," one girl jeered.

When the boy, Thorn, did his best to ignore her, someone else threw a rock. "Come on, tell us."

The rock caught Thorn squarely in the back; but though he grunted and straightened with the pain, he went right on cranking the bucket back up. Despite all the cuts and bruises I could see through the holes in his shirt, they still had not managed to beat the spirit from him. "I did see the Unicorn," he insisted.

"And why would the Unicorn appear to a kitchen servant?" laughed a woman. She was lounging by the well, waiting for her turn to draw up water. "He's one of the Five Masters who saved the world when all those monsters would have taken it over."

"You just saw a water buffalo and made the whole thing up," mocked a girl.

"No." Thorn lifted the well bucket onto the mouth of the well. "He had a horn growing right from the middle of his forehead and he was shining white."

"Humph." The woman jerked her head at him contemptuously. "Everyone knows the Unicorn is blue. If you're going to lie, at least make up a good one."

At first I was inclined to agree with the woman that the boy was a liar; but then I watched him pour the water from the well bucket into his own as if each drop was liquid gold instead of mere water.

His was an attitude of believing that even the smallest, most menial things must be done well. We try to develop just that same kind of spirit when we're young; but it's rare among humans—let alone in a young kitchen servant.

"Yes." I couldn't help speaking out loud. "There's still a touch of a unicorn's light to him."

The woman began to lower the well bucket again. "And what do you know about it, you old beggar?" And she spat at me.

The children turned toward me as a new target to mock. I would have liked nothing better than to change back to my true form and snap off a few of their monotonous little heads; but I knew I could not—even if stones were thrown. I did not even dare to use my staff to defend myself. If I did not want to frighten off Civet, I would have to swallow my pride and turn my back like a helpless old woman.

Preparing for the worst, I reminded myself that I had met worse insults and indignities in my years of wandering. After all, my pride should mean less to me than catching Civet.

But suddenly Thorn threw the bucket of water onto the other children. Even if he would not defend himself, he *would* protect an old beggar.

Shrieking, the children backed away, leaving the woman to stand alone as she wrung her hands in the air because some of the water had also splashed on her. "Your master, Knobby, is going to beat you for this, you treacherous little viper."

And, grabbing him by the ear, she marched Thorn down the street, followed by a mob of wet, cheering children until they all jammed into the inn.

I simply stood where I was, frozen with amazement. In all the years that I've wandered in disguise among humans, it was the first kindness that any one of them had ever done me. If I had been sensible, I would have left the village right then and waited outside to catch Civet. But I found it hard to turn my back on my little benefactor.

Picking up the bucket he had dropped, I filled it again, and then, with my staff in my other hand, I walked back to the inn.

From the courtyard, I could hear the triumphant voices of the wet woman and children laughing as a man's angry voice boomed. "That's the thanks I get for taking you in." There was the sound of a bamboo rod hitting flesh. "You've been trouble ever since that wandering peddler left you." Another smack. "I should have gotten rid of you long ago." But though it sounded as if the man—I suppose it was Knobby— was striking the boy as hard as he could, the boy did not cry out at all.

I did not want to become involved in another scene, so I followed an alley between the inn and a neighboring house until I found myself in a narrow space between the rears of the buildings and the village wall. The inn's back door was open—probably because of the heat of the day.

I found myself looking into a kitchen that was a rectangle eight meters long by five meters wide. A large pantry stood in the corner beside rows of large earthenware jars and shelves filled with smaller jars and bottles and plates and cups. A big, rectangular brick stove filled most of one wall. The soot from all the fires had completely blackened the wall and ceiling above it.

Setting the bucket of water to the right of the doorway, I sat down on the left side with my staff across my lap and with my back against the wall. I had learned long ago when dealing with humans never to turn my back to them and always to keep the exit within easy reach.

When Thorn finally came into the kitchen, he was breathing in short, sharp gasps, as if that helped him hold back the pain. Even so, he managed to ask, "Who are you?"

"You may call me Shimmer." I leaned forward to stare at him intently. "And I want to know why you helped me even when you knew you were going to take a beating for it."

"I'm used to beatings." He tried to shrug and winced at the pain.

There was something sharp and shining and hard to his spirit—like the blade of a fine steel sword. "But why take one more?" I demanded.

He took a small jar from a set of shelves near the stove. "You believed me when I said that I had seen the Unicorn." He smiled with one corner of his mouth. "Most people seem to take it for granted that an orphan automatically has to be a liar."

"Oh, come now," I said skeptically. "Someone here must have been kind to you."

"No one that I can remember." He squatted down in front of me. "But I'm not asking you for pity," he warned me. "I'm just stating the facts."

"Of course," I was quick to agree. But I couldn't help thinking that his spirit was wasted here—rather the way a good sword is dulled by using it to chop wood.

He presented the jar to me. "Would you mind putting some of this salve on my cuts?"

"Not at all." I took the jar from him.

Taking off his shirt, he turned around to reveal a back crossed and crisscrossed by the marks of many other beatings. "If it hadn't been for you and the Widow, I would have begun to think that I had made up the whole thing."

Though I tried to daub the salve on gently, Thorn

still flinched at my touch. "Who's this Widow?" I asked.

Thorn squirmed as if I were tickling him, and he leaned his arms on top of his knees. "Her husband was a miller, but now that he's dead, she's going to live with her sister in Edgewood. She told me that I must truly be blessed to have seen a unicorn."

And, as I spread the salve on his back, he enthusiastically described the Widow. She was the only guest staying at the tiny inn, which was just as well, since her attendants filled the rooms. Not only did she have the chair bearers and the guard, but she also had a pair of servants. "It's a funny thing about her though," Thorn mused. "Why would a woman dress in an expensive gown of green silk and at the same time wear such a cheap piece of jewelry?"

As I clinked the lid back onto the jar, I couldn't conceal my excitement. "Jewelry?"

Thorn twisted around and took the jar from me. "It's just a blue pebble." He shook his heard warningly. "It's not worth stealing, if that's what you're thinking."

I managed to keep from smiling. The pebble that

the boy dismissed so casually contained the waters of my lost sea home. "I was just curious," I said.

I began to run over the geography of the area. Lying about three hundred kilometers to the southeast, Edgewood was the nearest human village to the forest of the Keeper, a wicked old wizard in his own right. Perhaps she was traveling there to propose some alliance for more mischief.

If that was the case, she couldn't tell the humans that she was going there. No human would willingly enter his ancient forest. However, the story about the sister would cover her progress until the last possible moment, when she would turn away from human villages entirely. Until that time she could travel in disguise.

I tried to decide where would be the best place to meet Civet for our battle. It would have to be at least a few kilometers from the village, of course, where the villagers would not be able to help her.

I hadn't been too impressed by the glimpse I'd had of her guard. It would take more than him and her bearers and servants to stop me.

I was startled from my thoughts when Thorn said, "Thank you." He had just noticed the bucket of water.

"It was the least I could do." I took my staff from my lap and slowly began to rise.

"Where are you going?" He put a hand to my shoulder and pushed me back down. "Everyone in Amity will be coming here to listen to the Widow tell us the latest news." He walked over to an earthenware jar by the stove and began to pour the water into it. "There'll be enough scraps of food for both of us to have a regular feast."

"I should really be moving on," I observed, but I was touched by the boy's offer, since he was such an underfed, scrawny little thing. "You should keep all the food you can get."

"My stomach wouldn't know what to do with a full meal." He finished pouring the water into the jar and set the bucket down. "It might accuse me of overworking it. So why don't you stay?"

It had been ages since I had met such generosity, so I did not know how to refuse. "My thanks to you." I started to struggle to my feet. "Perhaps I can help you by chopping up some vegetables."

"No, no." He took a knife down from its nail. "You're my guest tonight." A king could not have smiled more graciously.

It was only a little after sunset when the first villagers began to crowd into the inn. In a small village like this, any traveler was a cause for excitement.

I was wondering if I shouldn't perhaps wait outside, but Knobby never came into the kitchen. It was up to Thorn to take the orders, do the cooking and serve the warm wine and bowls of noodles—though the trays were almost as large as he was.

But there certainly were plenty of scraps for us, just as he had predicted. I doubted if the boy had ever had so much in his life—or ever would again.

But my mind was only half on the meal as my ears strained to listen to the Widow tell them in a voice as cold as a mountain stream about the troubles in the land—riots, bandits, strange creatures stirring out of the shadows of ancient forest and mountain.

"Wait till there's a person of the proper blood on the throne," declared Knobby. "Then things will be set to right."

Twelve years ago the King had died in the northern wastes, driving back a huge war band of horse raiders. The Queen and her child had disappeared, and their general had claimed the throne instead. He had been apprenticed to a meat seller before he had joined the army, so he had been nicknamed the Butcher. Since he had gained the throne, he had lived up to that reputation by the ruthless slaughter of friends and foes alike. And the whole country was going to ruin.

Thorn, who had been sitting with his head cocked to one side to hear better, made a face. "That's what the talk always turns to—when there's a true king or queen—as if they could work miracles."

"Anything would seem better than the Butcher," I said. "He's surrounded himself with thieves and rascals who help him squander the treasury."

"Don't you start in too." Thorn looked bored.

"Yes, well"—I patted my stomach and got up—"my thanks to you, Thorn. This full belly ought to carry me a long way down my road."

Thorn paused in the act of picking up a vegetable stalk. "But it's too cold outside for bones as old as yours. Why don't you sleep here by the stove? It's always nice and warm."

I knew that I should leave to scout out some site for an ambush; but in all my travels, I had never met with such hospitality. After centuries of cold words and angry kicks, it seemed nothing short of a miracle to meet someone who wanted to share what little he had with me. "What about you?" I wondered.

Thorn jerked a thumb behind him. "I have to sleep by the pantry to keep away thieves, so don't worry about me."

I felt it would be wrong to leave. Besides, I told myself, I could rest here for a bit—in the warmth, which *would* be nice for a change; and when Thorn was asleep, I could sneak away and still have plenty of time to find the right spot for my battle.

"Thank you." I nodded my head to him. "Perhaps I will stay for a bit."

It was well that I did.

CHAPTER THREE

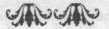

The moon rose bright and clear that night, slipping through the barred window and spilling across the floor in a long, striped rectangle almost like a tiger's pelt.

I knew it was time to be going, but I lingered for a few more minutes, savoring the warmth that the stove still gave off.

For one moment I felt as if I were small again, floating in the evenings beside my mother, washed all around by the warm waters of home—sometimes sleeping, sometimes gazing up at the stars ripening like fat pale cherries on a sheet of black velvet. Occasionally one of us would kick his legs, but most of the time we would drift along slowly, letting the lazy currents carry us about our inland sea.

It had been a lovely little sea and would be again, heaven willing, but it wasn't going to happen if I simply lay there, lost in my memories.

I was just about to get up when I heard someone bump into a table in the dining room. I hardly dared to breathe as the footsteps came toward the kitchen.

Raising one eyelid slightly, I saw the dim silhouette of a man standing in the doorway. At first I thought he was some enemy of mine, but he turned his head to stare at Thorn, who was sleeping several meters away, in front of the pantry.

I thought it was odd until I realized that the Unicorn was Civet's enemy—as were all creatures of goodwill. If the Unicorn had appeared to the boy once, he might come a second time and perhaps hear the gossip about the Widow with the blue pebble who was traveling to a place so close to the Keeper.

Maybe Civet had even placed one of her servants to eavesdrop on any conversations held in the kitchen.

If that was the case, she knew now that Thorn was willing to chat to perfect strangers, like myself, about the widow who had believed him. It was better to have the boy die during what appeared to be a robbery on the pantry than to leave him alive to bear tales to the Unicorn whenever he might visit next.

Civet's creature took another step. I told myself that it was sheer madness to defend a human boy. It was more important to take care of my own kind.

The creature slipped forward another meter, pausing on the very edge of the rectangle of moonlight. I knew that I ought to go after Civet now before she could slip away. Why should I waste the opportunity for which I and my entire clan had been waiting all these centuries?

Silently, the creature drew the cutlass from his sash. The moonlight shone on the blade so that it hung like a deadly, glittering smile. But the boy looked so helpless at the moment that I could not desert him. Besides, he had offered me bed and board, which made him my host.

The cutlass vanished from sight as the creature raised it upward into the darkness for one deadly stroke. But even as I sprang at the shadowy figure, I cursed myself for a fool and worse than a fool—a traitor to my own clan.

The creature and I tumbled sideways into the piles of pots, pans, bowls and plates that had been stacked on top of the stove to dry after being washed. Together we fell over with a clash and clatter loud enough for the end of the world.

"Thieves!" Thorn shouted at the top of his lungs. It would probably not be the first time someone had tried to get a free meal from the pantry. "Thieves! Wake up, everyone," Thorn yelled.

The creature staggered to his feet, slashing at the air, but I had my arms tightly about his neck. The only problem was that in my present disguise my legs and arms were too short to get a good grip, so I was slung about like a doll as he stumbled around the kitchen.

Even as a woman in the next room began to bawl out the alarm at the top of her lungs, Thorn appeared suddenly in the patch of moonlight. In his hand was a broad, heavy-bladed kitchen knife. It's just like humans to go charging in where they have no business to be.

"Stay back," I warned him.

After hesitating a moment, Thorn disappeared into the darkness. I couldn't see him at all, and the creature kept twisting and turning in circles to shake me from his back.

Then a fat, bowlegged man with a candle in one hand and a crossbow in the other came running into the kitchen. His thick eyebrows hung on the heavy ridge of his forehead, and I assumed that this was Knobby, the owner of the inn. "Stop where you are." He set the candle down on the floor and held up the crossbow. "I'm a deadly shot with this, the champion of four districts." But since he had forgotten to pull back the crossbow string, I had my doubts concerning his claim.

"Cock that crossbow," I snapped at him, "unless you're just trying to talk this thief to death." And tightening my grip on the creature's neck, I kicked down as hard as I could.

I must have caught the back of his knees—there was that much difference in our heights. He went down with a grunt, his head thudding sickeningly against a corner of the stove. And suddenly I was holding empty air while a little paper cutout floated gently down to the floor. The blow had destroyed the creature.

"Wait a moment. Wait a moment." Knobby was puffing away as he awkwardly cranked the crossbow string back.

"Never mind. He's gone." Wearily I got to my feet. I was sure that Civet, her chair and all of her servants would have vanished as well. "He was just a paper warrior."

"A what?" Knobby swung the crossbow toward me.

I pointed toward the cutout at my feet. "The Widow sent that thing to kill the boy."

"But why?" Knobby frowned, angry and puzzled.

"Because, for all she knew, he might have given her away to the Unicorn." I was suddenly feeling too tired to have to explain things to a human as dense as Knobby. "You'll find she's gone, leaving nothing but cutouts of servants and a sedan chair."

Knobby yelled over his shoulder for his wife to go check. She shouted back a moment later that everyone was gone. There were just pieces of paper littering the inn.

"It's witchcraft." Knobby swore and narrowed his

eyes. "Say, what are you doing here?" He aimed his crossbow at me as if a helpless old beggar woman was a target more to his taste.

"I felt sorry for her," Thorn explained, and gallantly stepped between Knobby and myself. "So I invited her to sleep here where it was warm."

Knobby lowered his crossbow and started to raise his hand for a backhanded slap at Thorn. "Worse than the thief from the street is the thief from your own household. I bet the two of you were feasting at my expense."

Well, I had just about had it with Master Knobby. Snatching up my staff from the floor, I thrust it over Thorn's head so that the tip was pointed at his master's snout.

When Knobby tried to duck under my staff, he still found the tip before his eyes. He tried to sidestep and then made several other moves, but I still held the staff unwaveringly in front of him. When he tried to raise his crossbow, I growled, "Don't try that, or I'll break that little thing you call a . . . a nose."

Knobby kept the crossbow aimed at the floor and swallowed. "On the other hand, who should forgo an act of charity?"

With one foot, I nudged Thorn to the side so that I had a clear field of action. "I'm sick of your kind." I scowled at him. "You water down the wine and skimp on the fillings in your meat pastries and you treat every small, weak creature shamelessly."

Knobby tried to draw himself up indignantly. "Now see here . . ." he began when I poked the tip of my staff against the bridge of his snout. His eyes crossed as he stared at the pole. "Ahem, yes, well, everyone has a right to their own opinion."

"What's going on here?" a woman demanded.

I turned to see a woman with stringlike hair. I supposed it was Knobby's wife. "We're just discussing certain regrettable business practices."

"Look out," Thorn cried and jumped past me. A crossbow string twanged and a bolt buried itself in the floor. Knobby had tried to shoot me while I was distracted by his wife; but Thorn had grabbed hold of his arm and deflected his shot.

"Why, you ungrateful little sneak." Knobby flung the boy against the wall.

"I've had just about enough of you." I swung my staff and gave him a good crack across the top of his head. Knobby slumped to the floor.

"Help, robbers, thieves!" Knobby's wife began screaming at the top of her lungs as she ran away.

I lowered my staff so that the boy could grasp the tip. "You saved my life," I said in surprise.

He grabbed hold of the tip and let himself be pulled to his feet. "Well, you saved mine."

This was a fine mess. I could hardly leave the boy behind to Knobby's tender mercies once he woke up. I would have to take the boy along with me—at least until we were far enough away from Knobby. "You'd better come with me," I said grimly.

He let go of my staff to dust off the seat of his pants. "But I've got five years to go on my bond."

I strode over to the stove. "You owe that fat bug nothing. Not from the first day that he took the bamboo rod to you." I picked up a knife and flint and handed them to him. "Here. Take these as your former master's gift to you."

Thorn held them stupidly on top of his palms. "But Amity's all that I've ever known."

"Humph," I snorted in disgust. "They say that you can open up the door to a tiger's cage, but you can't always make it leave."

"I'm not afraid." He tucked the flint and knife into

the sash he used as a belt. "We'll need these too."
He took down a bag and an empty gourd with a
strap attached to it.

"We're making our getaway, not planning an expe-
dition." I waved to him urgently from the rear doorway. "Why do you people always want to load
yourselves down with so much luggage that you can
hardly even walk?"

"Maybe *you* can eat and drink air, but I can't."
The boy quickly dumped some leftovers into the bag
and filled the gourd with water. Slinging the straps
over his shoulder, he started toward me. "All right.
I'm ready."

CHAPTER FOUR

We slipped out of the kitchen through the back door and crossed the narrow space to the high village wall. I held my staff about a half meter high and parallel to the ground. "Climb up on this."

Thorn hesitated about stepping onto the staff, glancing at my puny arms. Though I had helped him to his feet with the staff, it was quite another thing for me to support his full weight. It was obvious that he didn't think I could do it.

"Hop on," I urged with a nod of my head, "before the village finds out about us."

Thorn raised his foot high enough to test the staff and stared at me when it proved to be as rigid as the branch of a thick tree.

"You're not really an old woman, are you?" He narrowed his eyebrows suspiciously. "Are you a witch?"

"Wash your tongue with soap," I snapped at him. "I have never been a witch. They're to the magical arts what pickpockets are to banking." I didn't give him time to ask any more questions. "Up you go," I said, and started to raise the staff. He almost slipped off before he brought his other foot up and set his hands against the wall to steady himself. Then he was finally scrambling onto the top of the village wall.

With a short hop, I joined him there. "Hold on to one end of the staff," I instructed him. This time he obeyed me without a moment's hesitation, and I lowered him to the ground outside among the orchard trees that surrounded that side of the village. Then, throwing the staff away, I jumped down beside him, landing on my feet. I was off and running before he could even take a breath.

"Come on." I waved to him before I was hidden by the trees.

Somewhere in the village someone had begun beating the alarm gong, and people were shouting to one another. They seemed to think it was some kind of bandit raid. It would take them a while to sort out what was actually happening.

When we had reached the bottom of the hill, I held up my hand and then stopped. There was no one about in the field. "Good," I grunted. "I should have the time to make the change."

"Change into what?" The boy stared at me. His hand went to the hilt of his knife. "Just who are you?"

I couldn't see any reason to stay in my disguise any longer, so I let my actions serve as my explanation.

I proudly stepped away from the trees. "My people are the oldest and best of all living creatures." I pressed my hand against my forehead, where my pearl was hidden, and then, drawing the ancient sign in the air, I mouthed the familiar words of the spell.

But the boy looked frightened when my toes and legs began to twitch. "Are you feeling sick?" He took a step forward to help me.

"Honestly," I snapped in exasperation, "don't you

have any sense of spectacle at all?" My voice quavered as the trembling passed up through my legs and into the rest of my body. "Keep back."

Suddenly I felt a sharp pain in the small of my back as my spine started to lengthen to its usual three-meter length. Then my head snapped up as my neck began to stretch, and my jaws ached as they swelled outward into a proper snout. The worst part of it was that my skin felt terribly dry and itchy as it hardened into scales, but I didn't dare scratch until my fingers had finished arching into claws.

The boy's astonished eyes almost bulged from his head. "You're a dragon."

"Not just *a* dragon," I corrected him stiffly. "Can't you see that I have the five claws of royalty?" I would have lifted one of my transformed feet in demonstration, but I could feel my shoulder blades suddenly begin to arch from my back.

Wanting to savor the moment, I looked over my shoulder to watch the bones curve outward gracefully, stretching my skin until it was a pale, silvery-green color with the scales marked only by iridescent curls. When I finally spread my wings, it looked as if thousands of little rainbows were chasing behind me.

The boy suddenly stepped around to press his snout against mine. "You may be a royal dragon," he said, as if to reassure himself, "but you have the same kind eyes."

"Kindness is only for fools." I roughly shoved him away. "And I'm seldom one of those."

"But—" he began to protest.

"Listen to me, boy." I wagged a claw at him. "Never let your guard down to anyone. Or they'll stab you in the back the first excuse they can get."

The gates banged open at that moment. I looked over the treetops up the slope to the top of the hill, where the torchlight glinted off knives and spears. Things could get serious if I let that mob surround me.

The boy must have come to the same realization. "You'd better fly away before they catch you."

I wriggled my shoulders to relax the muscles before I took off. I didn't want to get any cramps while I was in the air because I hadn't warmed up properly. "And what about you, boy?"

He spread out his hands from his sides. "I'll run."

I dug my forefeet into the rich, deep earth. "And let Knobby catch you?" I shook my head at him. "I'm more thorough about my rescues than that." I crouched down. "Now don't get the idea that I'm a flying ferryboat, but I can drop you off someplace far away from Amity."

At that moment I heard a great shout of alarm as they sighted me.

"Let's discuss the matter while we're in the air, shall we?" I stretched out my neck. "Hop on."

The boy glanced at me and then at the gathering crowd and then back at me again. "Anything would be better than Knobby," he said, and climbed onto the base of my neck.

"Wrap your arms and legs around me and hold on tight," I warned him. "My flying teacher always told me to jump toward the clouds like a tiger leaping toward its prey."

"I thought you were the one who was in such a hurry to leave," he said playfully. "Why do you want to keep on talking?"

"I was just trying to warn you." Tensing, I thumped my tail against the ground and sprang skyward. It had been a *long time* since I had been free of the earth. I gathered the air with the thin, tough hide of my wings and shoved it roughly toward the ground so that we could rise still higher. I beat my wings faster and faster, eager to be away from the dirt, hungry to be where the air was clean and sweet.

In the sudden exhilaration of flying I banked, sliding around until I was upside down, and then did several loops so that the world seemed to spin round and round my head.

"Careful," Thorn shouted.

The laughter came bubbling from me. "A dragon princess must *fly* like a dragon princess. If you want safety, find some stinking, plodding camel." And I cut another loop in the air before I righted myself.

The sky above us looked so clear and innocent, but I knew it wasn't. The air looked as smooth as a new piece of silk, but it was like an ocean with strong, turbulent currents.

When we reached the great winds, they filled the air with soft hissing noises. Like giant feathered serpents, they coiled around us—their featherlike touches unable to hide the hard, steely muscle beneath. If they could, they would have sent us tumbling back to the ground; but I wasn't any novice.

I wriggled, twisted and soared, hopping from the back of one wind to the back of another until I found one that was sweeping southeast. And there I settled with outstretched wings on its undulating back, riding the wind as it dipped and then rose and dipped again, following the contours of the ground beneath as we shot toward Civet.

CHAPTER FIVE

At first, I was so excited about flying with a dragon that I didn't really think about anything else. I had never been farther than Amity's fields—at least that I could remember. And now here I was soaring over the world itself.

The streams gleamed like silver ribbons in the moonlight, and the fields lay next to one another like old soft cotton patches, so that the whole countryside reminded me of a giant cotton quilt that had been thrown down.

But I had hardly begun to enjoy the flight when Shimmer asked, "Now, where do you want me to leave you, boy?"

Suddenly I had this terrible, hollow feeling inside—as if the dragon had plucked me from her neck and told me it was time for me to flap my arms and fly on my own.

As hard as my life had been with Knobby, at least I had always known who I was and what I was supposed to do. So the prospect of all that freedom was rather scary. "Can't I go with you?" I asked desperately.

"It's too dangerous, boy." Shimmer studied the stars overhead and then altered her course slightly. "That Widow is really a wicked creature called Civet. She stole my sea and put it into a blue pebble."

The cold wind blowing by my face was beginning to make my nose itch. "I've heard a tale about a witch doing that." I had only meant to show that I wasn't completely ignorant; but it was the wrong thing to say.

We dropped several meters through the air as Shimmer missed a beat of her wings. "It's a fine thing," she spluttered indignantly, "when the tragic history of your clan is reduced to a mere legend. You humans lead such short lives that the facts of one generation become the stories of the later ones. And for your information, she isn't a witch but the wife of a river spirit. She destroyed him some time ago and took over his spells and such. But though she *made some trouble for our friends at River Glen, we really didn't worry about her. And then she came one night and took away our sea."*

"I can't help it if I haven't lived as long as you." I tried to rub my nose against my shoulder to keep myself from sneezing.

"I suppose not," the dragon said grudgingly. She beat her wings harder and faster through the air as if the mere thought of Civet made her want to hurry on. "But now you know what's at stake. I intend to catch Civet no matter what I have to do—even if I have to change myself into a worm crawling across a pit of fire."

"Do you think it's really going to be that bad?" I was beginning to worry about my companion.

"Probably worse." Shimmer nodded toward a green spot on the horizon. "I think she's heading for the forest of the Keeper."

I had heard tales about a wicked wizard who had gotten that name because he kept a menagerie of monstrous pets. He used to enslave entire human villages; but I had thought he was only make-believe. "You mean," I asked cautiously, "he's real too?"

"Of course," she snapped, as if annoyed at my stupidity.

"Almost two thousand years ago he was a real wizard who knew too much magic for his or anyone else's good. Finally his slaves rose up against him and there was a terrible, desperate battle in which many of the slaves were slain. But all of his pets were killed and he had to use up most of his magic."

"The tales also said he was dead." I frowned.

"All tales have to have a happy ending." Shimmer's laugh was short and bitter. "Unfortunately, life isn't that way. The Keeper still had one last bit of magic left—a gem called the mist stone. He used its power to change himself into a cloud and escaped into an impregnable tower."

I didn't exactly enjoy the idea of heading into that kind of trouble, but I couldn't let her face Civet and the Keeper by herself. "Maybe I'd better go with you," I offered. "You might need help."

Though I was clinging to the base of her neck, it was still long and slender enough for her to twist her head to look at me with good-natured contempt. "You'd be next to useless. Why, I bet those teeth of yours couldn't even bite through a twig."

"I've got a knife," I said stubbornly.

Smugly, she raised a foot so I could see it. "Each of my

claws is longer and sharper than your kitchen knife."

Her boastful ways were starting to annoy me. "I'd still want as much help as I could get if I were you."

"I daresay," she sniffed. "Humans always have to be part of a mob before they feel brave."

That really got to me. "I saved your life when Knobby would have shot you."

However, my reminder only seemed to irritate her. "That's not the same thing as holding your own in a fair fight."

I felt as if someone ought to uphold the honor of the human race. "All right." I took a deep breath and let it out in a rush. "If I run away or hold you back, you can just leave me. But I'll never let you down. You just wait and see."

"That's a bold-enough promise," she scoffed, "but can you keep it?"

"You won't know," I pointed out, "unless you take me along."

Shimmer studied me with a cold, professional eye. "Listen to me, boy. You're trying to stay with me because I'm the only person you know outside of Amity. You don't really want to travel with me. You just think you do."

I suppose it was the truth, but I wasn't willing to admit

it. As I held on to her neck, I could feel her great muscles rippling beneath the hide of her shoulders. She seemed so strong and sure of herself that I felt safer with her than I ever had with anyone in Amity. And besides, the thought of being alone in the world seemed far more frightening than Civet and the Keeper—who still seemed partly imaginary.

"It won't do you any good to drop me off," I told her, "because I'll follow you on foot."

Shimmer frowned. "Don't be a fool, boy. It's not your fight."

"But it is my fight," I insisted. "After all, she tried to kill me."

Shimmer drew her heavy eyebrows together as if genuinely puzzled. "Humans don't usually take their feuds as seriously as dragons."

I knew that I had her: The tales said that dragons held their names and reputations dearer than their lives. A feud might go on for thousands of years and span several of their generations. At least the tales had been accurate about one thing. "I intend to pay Civet back," I said, trying to sound both bold and determined.

"You'll have to stand in line." Shimmer glanced up at

the stars and adjusted her course again. "Well, far be it from me to interfere when a creature feels its honor is at stake." She faced forward once more. "However, I'm afraid you're going to have a short—if busy—life with me."

CHAPTER SIX

My human, would-be champion and I reached the forest of the Keeper about an hour before sunrise. The trees grew so close together that their tops seemed like the green waves of an ocean frozen by some magic. "This used to be orchards and parks before the trees ran wild," I said.

"Are we near Civet?" the boy asked.

"If she's with the Keeper, then we're still probably several kilometers away." I scanned the treetops until I found a narrow clearing. "I want to surprise her if I can. I'll never do that trying to fly in directly. So hold on." I banked in the air, turning in a slow, ever-tightening spiral downward.

I landed with a kind of springy bounce like a cat. It wasn't bad considering how out of practice I was. I shook my neck for him to get off. "Let's get into our disguises right away."

"You mean I get one too?" the boy asked as he slid onto the ground.

"We can't have Civet recognizing you." I smiled wickedly. "Or she'll use her magic to blast you into cinders."

"Can I have big muscles and a sword?" he asked eagerly.

"We don't want to frighten her off either." I laughed, touching my forehead. My magical pearl was hidden there behind a fold of flesh, since there were many creatures who would have fancied the pearl my mother had willed to me. Muttering the words and making a sign, I made a quick little spell.

Instantly his limbs and body stretched, and he unhappily examined his bowlegs and thin, sallow arms. "This isn't quite what I had in mind."

"That's the way it is with magic." I touched my

pearl again and changed myself into a little old pilgrim. I couldn't help wriggling my shoulder blades. "The worst thing about having to go about as a human is that I get an itch right about where my wings should be."

Hurriedly, the boy reached up and scratched around my shoulder blades. "There, does that feel better?"

I squirmed and then settled down. "Much better," I sighed contentedly.

"You see," he said to me, "everyone needs someone—even if it's only to scratch their back."

But I didn't want him to get the wrong impression. "A tree branch makes a good back scratcher too—and it never expects compliments."

We traveled for about four kilometers before we reached the edge of the Keeper's ancient city. The boy halted almost immediately. "Where did that come from?" He pointed to a half-crumbled building that rose upward ahead of us.

"This is the Keeper's city." I waved a hand all around us. "Or rather, it was."

The building consisted of a half dozen terraces, each progressively smaller than the lower one so that the entire structure was shaped roughly like a pyramid. But trees grew from the cracked stones of the paving and vines strangled the upper levels, so the building seemed more like a shaggy green mound than a stone ruin.

Thorn rubbed his cheek thoughtfully. "How do you know we're going in the right direction?"

"The streets of his city were said to be laid out like the spokes of a wheel, with his tower at the very hub." I pointed down the green, shady avenue. "All we have to do is keep going straight."

Suddenly the boy whirled around. I couldn't help looking in the same direction, but there was no one about. Still, he rubbed the back of his head. "I keep getting the feeling that we're being watched."

"The people are long since ghosts." I shoved him along in front of me. "And his pets died during the fighting."

Though the streets had once been paved with stones, they were covered now with a thick carpet of leaves and dirt. Farther within the dead city a different species of trees grew, with roots that needed very little dirt, roots that oozed over dirt and stone like thick ropes.

But with each step, I began to feel the same eerie sensation as the boy. I turned to look behind us once again, but I couldn't see anything. I told myself that I shouldn't let the boy's wild imagination influence me.

I was just starting to get over my nerves when the boy gave a startled gasp. I whipped around to see a face staring at me from the trunk of a tree.

At first I thought it was a person in the tree, but then I realized that it was only a statue with a calm, puzzling smile. A tree was slowly growing around it, having covered everything except its face.

"Don't scare me so," I snapped and dragged the boy after me down the street. Statues had once lined either side, though the forest was slowly claiming each one. Many of the statues had been completely swallowed and the trees had taken on their shapes. But others, like the tree with the face, had not yet been taken over entirely. Occasionally I could see a marble hand or foot protruding from a tree trunk—as if the trees were partly human.

I began to have the feeling that the trees were even slowly reaching out for us. This was a city that belonged to the forest now—a forest that hated anything that moved. If we once stopped—if we even paused momentarily—the forest would gulp us down as well.

The deeper we went into the city, the denser the trees became, until they grew so close together that they seemed to form a solid wall on either side. More and more, the branches intertwined overhead until the sun was shut out completely. The only light came from glowing mosses that hung in pillowlike masses on the branches. We both kept ducking our heads trying to avoid the touch of the moss, which left a foul, oily stain.

Suddenly my heart nearly stopped when something rustled to our right. I searched the branches, but there was only the moss hanging like tattered shrouds. "It was probably only some lizard." I tried to laugh at my own foolish nervousness when something rustled on our left. "Or maybe it's two lizards." Or had the Keeper recovered enough of his powers to begin gathering a new menagerie of pets?

As we started forward cautiously, the leaves began to rustle all around us, and smaller, twiglike branches began to snap as if there were many unseen creatures keeping pace with us. Instinctively the boy and I drew together, moving almost in step.

I was so busy searching the trees for our secret companions that I never saw the tree root until I tripped over it.

"Are you all right?" Thorn eyed the tree anxiously.

"Yes." I sat up hurriedly. I can't say I was very happy at the ease with which my human shape bruised its shins, though. I looked at the street ahead of us and gave a worried grunt. The roots of the trees covered the entire street now like a snarled mess of giant yarn. "It's always so pleasant to take a little stroll."

From behind us came a loud, evil hoot as if there were some large, malicious owl watching us from hiding. "It's probably only some harmless bird," I reassured Thorn—though I, for one, didn't particularly enjoy the prospect of meeting it.

"Or you hope it's only a bird." He slipped the knife from his sash as a precaution.

"Well, perhaps we shouldn't wait around to find out." I got up hurriedly. And for once the boy was quick to nod his head in agreement.

But as we walked on, the moss began to appear upon the trunks of the trees and even on the roots themselves, so that if we didn't trip on the roots, we were just as likely to slip on the slimy moss.

Worse, the trees began to close in until the street became a narrow tunnel of living wood a meter wide and two meters high. I felt almost as if the forest itself were swallowing us and we were making our way down its long, twisting throat. Suddenly we could no longer see the trees up ahead. There was only a wall of moss giving off a sickly, ugly glow.

"It looks like we've come to a dead end." I looked at the moss without much enthusiasm. "Maybe we'd better retrace our steps."

Instantly the branches shook behind us and a shower of leaves fell as a spiderlike creature dropped down on a strong yet slender string. The beast was about a meter long, and its short fur was banded in gold and black and covered its round head—though it also had the large, staring eyes and beak of an owl. It opened its beak and gave the same disturbing hooting we had heard before.

A rubbery centipede with a bristly back and mantis-like claws crept down a nearby tree trunk, leaving an eerily lit trail in its wake across the moss. Farther back, I could see the shape of a larger creature step out onto the roots. But it was too far away in the dim light to make out its features. A second large shape joined it. And it seemed as if there were more in the shadows behind them—though I could not be sure.

In the narrow space between the tree trunks, I really wouldn't have room to maneuver in a fight, so I was glad when Thorn gave a shout. "I don't think there's anything behind the moss. Just let me kick this stuff away."

Bright light suddenly spilled down the lane, and the centipede scuttled halfway back toward the branches while the spider creature blinked its eyes. I glanced behind me to see Thorn widening a narrow gap between two trees. "I can see some kind of building in front of us. And a circle."

It sounded just like the space I needed for a battle. I turned back to the creatures. They were coming on slowly. "Go on then." I shoved the boy ahead of me through the moss and plunged after him a moment later in the open light and air.

I scrambled quickly to my feet and found we had stumbled into a large circle of some black crystal in which faint streaks of red and yellow and white gleamed like the flames of a fire seen through badly distorted glass. The streaks seemed to flicker slowly, as if the fire were burning in slow motion.

Thirty meters away, at the very center of the circle, was a tall cylindrical tower of the same material. Forty meters in diameter at its base, the tower rose some fifty meters into the air, tapering slightly at the roof. There didn't seem to be one crack or blemish in its smooth, polished surface except for a large window at the very top.

"That must be the Keeper's tower," I said.

There was an answering chorus of hoots and growls from behind us as a dozen of the Keeper's pets burst from the gap to form a wall on either side of us. The centipede remained behind in the gap itself. We could now only go forward to the black tower itself.

CHAPTER SEVEN

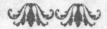

A large stone slab at the base of the tower slid upward silently; and a tall, elderly stick of a man stepped out. The top of his head had been shaved so that it almost gleamed in the bright light, but his white hair grew long from the sides of his head all the way down to his shoulders. His head looked rather like a giant egg to which someone had attached an old, faded grass skirt.

His wraparound robe must have been magnificent at one time, but it now hung in baggy folds on his long, thin frame. Red thread had been sewn into its black silk to create a pattern that looked uncomfortably like a series of grasping claws. They seemed to writhe and snatch at things all over his robe. The one single ornament on his robe was a round gold setting that must have once held a jewel over his heart. But the jewel was missing.

"What an unexpected pleasure," he said in a tight, twisted voice like a vine slowing strangling a tree. "After all these centuries, I've suddenly become very popular again."

"I hope we haven't disturbed you." I craned my neck trying to look inside his tower, but I did not see Civet.

"Not at all, my dear sir." His eyes glittered as cold and calculating as a snake about to strike. "I rather welcome the excuse to rest from my labors." He nodded behind us. "As you can see there is much to restore."

I glanced around us. "And so many pets to tend."

He held out his hands from his sides. "It's been a while since I had the resources to feed my pets properly." He looked beyond us toward his creatures. "And my little group is still only a fraction of what it once was. But soon . . ." His words faded into an ugly chuckle. "In any event, it's rather thoughtful of you to provide lunch for my pets."

Thorn started to slide the bag of food from his shoulder. "I don't think it's going to go far among them, but you're welcome to what we have."

The Keeper clasped his hands behind his back and leaned his head forward like some giant vulture. "That wasn't what I had in mind."

I turned my head to Thorn. "He means he's going to feed us to those things." I touched my hand to my forehead. "Or so he thinks." A quick sign and a murmured spell and our outlines began to waver.

The Keeper's pets drew back, hooting and screeching in alarm; but by the time we had finally solidified into our true shapes, the Keeper had recovered from his momentary surprise.

"I had no idea I had a dragon as a guest." He glanced at my feet. "And a royal one at that." He gave a deep bow. "I'm honored." When he straightened up, he frowned intently. "Your markings, though, seem rather strange to me, unless . . . Yes"— he wagged his index finger at me—"you're a daughter of the Lost Sea."

I clicked my claws against the black crystal. "Then a clever fellow like yourself will also understand why I'd be interested in Civet. Has she visited here recently?"

"She's been here with some wild plan to destroy a city called River Glen." He lifted one shoulder. "She said she used to live there at one time." The Keeper touched the empty golden setting on his robe. "But she's gone now—and stolen something of great value to me."

"The mist stone?" I asked.

"Yes." The Keeper winced at the memory of his recent loss. "I sent some of my pets after her. But she's eluded them so far."

I could feel a chill pass down from my spine all the way from the tip of my tail up to my skull. He would need a substitute for the mist stone now, and a dragon's pearl could power a variety of spells. So my pearl was just as valuable to him as his own gem. I touched a foot to my forehead involuntarily.

"Yes," he smiled, as if reading my thoughts. "It's so kind of you to bring me a replacement for my stolen treasure."

"But I won't be able to work any magic without

the pearl," I said, trying to buy time while I dropped my foot and tensed my legs.

He smiled with a self-satisfied air. "But you won't have much choice—" His sentence ended in a sudden yelp as I leaped for him. Unfortunately for me, he stumbled backward through the doorway, so that my jaws closed only on empty air. Before I could gather myself for another spring, the slab had dropped down.

"Watch out," Thorn shouted. Waving his knife over his head as if it were some cutlass, he stepped in between myself and a charging cat-headed scorpion. I suppose the Keeper's pets had been frightened by the suddenness of my transformation rather than the fact that I was a dragon.

With a lunge I stretched a forefoot around the boy and raked at the creature. It skipped back just in time to avoid being laid open.

"You see," Thorn crowed to me, "I really can be helpful." But in order to save me, the little fool had deliberately turned his own back upon a six-legged bear that was just about to swat him.

I knocked the bear away with a sweep of my tail. "Don't you have any sense at all?" I raged at the boy. "Always protect yourself first in a fight."

"But we're a team." The boy sliced a few times at the air.

"Let me explain a few facts to you, boy." A kick from my hind leg sent a tiger-headed creature backward with a yowl. "We are not a team." I whipped my tail at the owl-faced spider. "To be a teammate you must be an equal partner." I took another swipe at the bear. "But I have to protect both you *and* myself."

His face fell as if I had struck him. "All right then. I'll try to keep them away while you go after the Keeper." He raised his knife and faced the nearest clump of pets.

He was an even bigger fool if he thought he could keep the monsters away for more than a second. Still, he was a brave fool and an unselfish one—neither of which I had encountered very often among humans. I wished his arm could match the strength of his heart. He deserved a better fate than becoming another free meal for the Keeper's pets.

"Oh, quit the heroic poses," I pretended to grumble. "I don't have time to carve a monument for you." Plucking him up by his collar, I tossed him onto the back of my neck.

"But I told you to go on," the boy protested.

I whirled in a circle, sweeping my tail around to clear a large space. "I can't get at the Keeper once he's inside his tower. And besides, Civet is the one we really want." I gnashed my teeth together menacingly toward several creatures who seemed to be working up their nerve to charge. "Have you got a good grip?" I called to the boy.

"I think so," Thorn said.

"Then here we go." I sprang into the air, immediately spreading out my wings and flapping them so that we began to fly upward past the slick sides of the tower.

The winds almost seemed to be waiting for me above the tower roof. Strong and sinewy, they felt almost solid enough to sink my claws into their backs. Desperately I stretched my wings so that winds could sweep us away. They were blowing to the west—all the better, since River Glen lay in that direction. When we reached the city, we would also find Civet.

"Is that another of the Keeper's pets?" Thorn wondered.

I glanced below us to see an ape-headed fly suddenly emerge from the tower window. The Keeper followed a moment later on the back of a wasp-winged creature with the antlers of a deer and the swordlike beak of a crane.

"Yes," I said grimly, "and they'll be hunting *us* now."

CHAPTER EIGHT

We shot westward over a wide stretch of hills that looked almost like a green carpet that had just been unrolled so that it still had its curves and bumps. By sunset we had reached the Desolate Mountains, whose steep ranges had been raised when the Serpent Lady had conquered the underground Earth Lords at the very beginning of the world. The sinking sun seemed to turn the snowcapped peaks into a fleshy orange-red like newly peeled rinds.

"They're gaining," Thorn said.

I glanced behind me and saw that it was true.

"How long can you keep flying?" he asked.

"As long as they can." I paused and then added, "I hope."

The real trouble began once we entered the mountain ranges, which lay like half-healed scars on the earth. Each range seemed to grow steeper, so that I was forced higher and even higher into the thinner, almost freezing air. My wings began to feel numb from the cold, and yet I had to try to beat them faster because the thinner air did not support our weight as well.

And though I flapped my wings until they ached, the black dots drew steadily closer. "They're certainly nimble little creatures, aren't they?"

Thorn pointed ahead of us. "Say, what's that?"

I turned to the front again. The newly risen moon made the horizon shine in a dazzling white arch like the freshly cleaned rib of some unfortunate corpse. "It's the Lost Sea," I murmured. "My former home. I was away when Civet stole the sea and I haven't been back since then." I flew on for several beats before I added, "The water's all gone now, but most of the salt's still there—except for some that got into the pebble. Civet's destination is beyond it, so we're going the shortest route." And, I thought, I should be able to fly faster because I could fly lower there.

My wingbeats grew stronger and surer and my heart exulted because I was going home again. The seafloor seemed to swell until it was a broad, flat oval that seemed to collect the moonlight and reflect it back in shimmering waves like a porcelain plate new from the kiln fires.

Home. The word was a chant within my heart that helped me to shed all the weary years and kilometers, all the sullen faces and angry words, all the sorrows and disappointments of the roads. I was going home.

With each stroke of my wings, the Lost Sea widened ahead of us until it almost filled the entire horizon. Only the peaks of the last mountain range edged its eastern border. Eagerly my eyes began to search the whiteness for old, familiar landmarks.

Instead, I saw a dozen black specks suddenly rise from the seafloor. They shot upward, easily cutting us off. As we neared them, I could see that their wings were curved like the blades of scythes, and I knew with a growing sense of dismay that they were probably the search party the Keeper had mentioned he would send after Civet. It would be logical to send them to the Lost Sea, since it was the most direct route to River Glen. They probably had orders to intercept any large creature. I had let myself be driven into another trap.

I craned my neck around. The Keeper was only twenty meters away, riding on the back of his wasp-winged pet while a dozen other different creatures surrounded him protectively. "Surrender now," the Keeper yelled, "and I'll see that your deaths are painless."

A hawk-headed creature shot by overhead, turning in a slow, predatory circle. Another creature flew below us, and still more darted by on our left and right.

"They've boxed us in," Thorn said, frightened.

"Much to their regret." I stretched out my wings like an army unfurling its banners. "They'll find that a dragon princess doesn't die easily." I took a quick, deep breath so that the thick, corded muscles of my chest and shoulders stood out. And then, shouting the great war cry of my clan, I drew in my wings and dove through the air.

"After her," the Keeper shouted desperately, and with shrill cries his pets dove after me.

I curled in my head and tail until my back was to the ground. Then I arched my wings. When I was in practice, I never had any trouble with the maneuver. But it had been a long time since I had last been able to fly in combat maneuvers. I felt now as if the weight of the entire world had suddenly fallen on my back and shoulders. I winced at the sharp pains in my wings and I wondered if the bones would snap. I tightened the muscles of my chest and belly as I fought to beat my wings and break our fall.

Above us, the Keeper and his pets were still plunging downward, their wings folded in and their claws stretched out like sea divers. They seemed like strange fruit hanging in the air and growing larger and larger with each moment. The Keeper was staring down at me, his eyes widening in surprise at my trick.

And then they were all around us. Unfortunately, the Keeper was too far away, but I managed to strike at a good number of his pets. My tail, wings, claws and teeth beat and tore at them while the poor creatures, still caught in the momentum of their dive, didn't have the time to strike at me before they had gone past.

For a moment I felt as young and energetic as a

dragon newly hatched from its egg. I almost felt as if there was nothing I could not do. With one great beat of my wings I went soaring upward.

Beneath us I could hear the snapping of wing bones and screams as the Keeper's pets tried to turn in tight loops to rise after me. But their flimsy little wings weren't meant for such maneuvers—well, neither were mine when they were flabby.

"Two of them are falling," Thorn shouted triumphantly.

"And a good many more to go." The first wave of pets had been our immediate pursuers, but the other pets were closing in now.

I didn't wait to see any more but did a sharp barrel roll that sent me downward again. There were a half dozen pets immediately beneath me, but the Keeper was farther away since his own pet had done a safer, looser loop. He stared up at me with a frightened, bloodless look, and then he kicked his mount into a sharp dive as if he were determined to put as much distance between himself and me as he could.

Then I was among his pets once more. My claws ripped through the thin leather of wings and my teeth tore at feather and fur. But their claws and beaks and fangs found their marks as well. I could feel a half dozen new cuts on my body as I did a slower, wider loop away.

By that time the Keeper had called in all of his pets to form a protective screen between himself and me.

He was now about forty meters below me. "I once heard of a certain young dragon princess," he called. "It was said that no one was quite her match when it came to flying and fighting."

"Did you?" I leveled off, glancing all around me as my flying instructor had taught me to do.

"In fact, the tales said that she hadn't come of age so she hadn't been given her pearl yet to power her spells." His voice had taken on a sly note. "But being impetuous and greedy, she tried to steal the dream pearl, which had the additional power to create any number of illusions. Unfortunately for her she was almost caught, so she was forced to run away with it."

"Oh?" I felt compelled to correct him. "And I heard that her mother had promised the pearl to her; but when the mother died, her brother tried to claim it instead."

The Keeper also leveled off, careful to keep his pets still between us but making no move to attack. Apparently he was unsure of his own ability to beat me in an aerial battle.

"Personally," he shouted up to me, "I've always felt that magic belongs to the strongest. So it was rather foolish to banish her. She might very well have been able to stop Civet from stealing the sea."

"And then again"—I circled warily—"she might not."

"Neither she nor I have much reason to love Civet." He slipped his hands behind his back. "If you know where to find this poor unfortunate outlaw, we might make an alliance against Civet. I could show her how to use her pearl to cast illusions. And that way I could regain my gem and she could restore her sea."

I had learned long ago never to trust a magician when you cannot see his hands—especially when he seems to be talking fair, reasonable words. So I was glad of the boy's company. An extra pair of eyes might save our lives. "Keep a sharp lookout," I murmured to the boy, and then called down to the Keeper, "Why should you want to help her?"

"I could very well waste my resources fighting her," the Keeper explained. He had kept his own pets moving, so that the distance remained the same. "Her own people are homeless now, but it must be even harder for her. As an outlaw she can't go among the other dragons. In fact, she can't even keep her own true shape because there would always be some unscrupulous person trying to steal the dream pearl."

"Yes, there probably would." I glided through the air, belly taut, my whole body as rigid as a dagger blade as I studied the pets' formation.

The Keeper's voice became just a little too sweet. "But if she could capture Civet, she would become a hero who would be welcome everywhere, and the dream pearl would officially be hers."

One hand was hidden behind his mount's head, but I was sure he was working magical signs. "And she could have all that if she cooperated with you?"

"Oh, yes." He nodded quickly. He was too far away for me to hear the spell, but his lips were moving in a chant.

I decided that if I could just break through his screen of pets, I could catch him. However, my chances would be better if I could draw just a bit closer to him. It was time to distract him a little. "But the pearl is such a lovely thing that you might just want to keep it." And I put a foot to my forehead and pulled back the fold of flesh so that the pearl could rise outward.

The pearl was small—only about the size of the boy's thumbnail—so it would be easy to miss when it was covered. But exposed now, it emitted a soft light that seemed to swirl around us, sometimes silver, sometimes a metallic blue or green or red like the inside of an abalone shell.

The Keeper's pets hissed and squawked in alarm, but the Keeper merely stared up at me. "It's as lovely as they say," he said admiringly. "I—I mean, we could create all sorts of illusions: phantom armies, giant monsters . . ." His voice drifted off as he no longer had words for the scope of his vision.

He was off to my left but only twenty meters below me now. It was just close enough. "In short, every nightmare that your warped mind is capable of."

"Don't be a fool," he said in angry disbelief. "You could have whatever you wanted. Your kingdom. Your clan."

"I don't want them your way." Covering the pearl

and folding my wings, I gave the war cry of my clan and dove in a steep slant toward him.

I wasn't a moment too soon, because the Keeper threw up his hands almost at the same instant. There was a strange sizzling sound and the air suddenly grew warm behind us and the stars disappeared from overhead.

"There's a giant net right where we were," Thorn cried. "And it's all on fire." I suppose the Keeper had decided it would be easier to take the pearl from my corpse. Thorn added shrilly, "And the net's following us."

"Ha! He's outfoxed himself this time." Pulling in my tail, I began to beat my wings, hoping to add to the speed of our dive. "If we can just keep ahead of it a little longer, we can trap him in it instead."

Below us, the Keeper's pets flapped their wings and made frightened sounds as they circled in confusion, blinking their eyes as if blinded by the bright glare of the net that was falling behind us. Beneath them, the Keeper began to make frantic signs as if he were going to make the net disappear.

I darted straight through the middle of the pets' formations. None of them moved to intercept me;

but by chance a pet drifted in front of me. Instinctively it reached out its claws to drive me away. Ducking my head, I banked sharply and felt a sudden pain in my left wing as I made a ninety-degree turn, beating my wings as fast as I could to take us away.

I caught a glimpse of the Keeper as we turned. He had given up trying to make the net disappear, and instead was trying to get his own mount to bank downward and away from the falling net.

It was only when we had cleared the last of the Keeper's pets that I dared to look at the net myself. It easily spread for some twenty meters on each side and seemed to fill the sky with a fine, burning mesh. Even as I watched, the giant net draped itself about the Keeper's pets. For a moment they hung there with wings spread out like strange, terrible ragged butterflies of light. And then the net was dropping through the air with terrible speed.

The Keeper yelled out in pain as the edge of the net caught him. His mount twisted frantically, trying to get free, but it was snared. I waited for the net to vanish, but perhaps there just wasn't time or perhaps the net kept him from making the proper signs.

I supposed we would never know. We could only

watch as the brightly burning net fell from sight until it was only a fiery little point of light that winked out once it touched the white floor of the Lost Sea.

Then it was dark. And the stars, hidden momentarily by the fiery net, reappeared once more.

"You did it," the boy shouted to me. "You did it!"

"But for how long?" I would have liked to do some victory loops, but the pain had grown steadily worse in my left wing. I pulled it in with a jerk. And as we began to drop through the air, I craned my neck and saw the great slash standing red and bloody on the skin of my wing.

It seemed as if our victory over the Keeper was going to be a rather short one.

I tried to beat my wings to break our fall, but the pain was too great and I couldn't seem to beat them fast or hard enough. The wind whistled by our ears as we fell, and the white plain below seemed to leap up toward us.

"Come on," I muttered to myself. "You're not going to give up now." I could feel the boy tighten his arms around my neck as, with one last determined effort, I began to flap my wings frantically. A small cloud of white salt rose from underneath us. My injured wing almost felt as if it were on fire. But we began to slow in the air. Even so, we landed with a jarring thump.

...
...
...
...

CHAPTER NINE

I was thrown off Shimmer when we landed. At first I thought the cracking noises were our bones breaking. But when I opened my eyes, I saw all the cracks radiating outward across the surface of the seafloor. The weight of our bodies had shattered the smooth expanse of salt.

Shimmer heaved herself up on her forelegs and almost slipped as the salty chunks crumbled even more beneath her. "Nothing feels broken." She tested each of her legs in turn. Then she caught sight of the large red drops staining the salt. "Is that my blood?"

"It's from that cut on your wing." I got up slowly, still trying to get my breath back.

Shimmer craned her neck around and gradually spread her wings outward to reveal a gash as long as my forearm. "I'm sure it's going to leave a scar," she almost pouted. "Up till now my wings have always been my best feature."

I tried to take a step toward her and fell as the salt blocks broke into smaller bits. "Can't you heal it with some spell so that it doesn't leave a mark?"

"I don't want to go around using magic frivolously." Hurriedly she raised her wing—as if wanting to avoid any more questions. "Maybe it just looks worse than it is." She tried to flap her wings and winced at the pain. "No, that won't do."

But I was curious now about some of the things that the Keeper had said, so I made my way over to her with elaborate care. "Can't you at least cast a healing spell?" I asked.

She gave a little embarrassed cough. "You have to understand that my education was cut short by that misunderstanding over the pearl." She added weakly, "I had just worked my way through the theory of magic and was getting down to actual spells like changing my shape and size when I . . . um . . . had to leave.''

I steadied myself by leaning against her shoulder. "Are those the only spells you know?" I challenged her.

She thrust her face against mine. "I'd like to see you do better.''

But she didn't seem quite so impressive now. "Just how old were you when you were exiled?" I demanded suspiciously.

"I was all of three hundred years old." She shifted her hind legs uneasily, breaking the salty surface with more loud snaps.

But I wasn't about to let her off the hook. "You're just a child, then, as dragons go," I said in an annoyed voice. "So even if you're a good flier and fighter, you don't know much about magic." My sullen mood wasn't helped any by the salt that was stinging the back of my neck. "And you probably never had lessons in real tactics either. You just charged right into the Keeper's traps."

"And I got us out of them, didn't I?" She gave a quick, firm nod of her head.

But as the old proverb goes: Plant a seed of doubt; harvest a field. I couldn't help wondering how many other half-truths she had told me. "All right. But I don't understand why you stole the pearl if you don't know much magic."

"Because it was my mother's," she insisted defensively. "And because it had been promised to me. My brother would have kept it locked away in a vault. He didn't care about all those lovely afternoons swimming alongside our mother while she conjured up all those marvelous illusions." Shimmer smiled slightly at the memory. "The ancient heroes of old, the icy palaces of the north glittering like diamonds— Mother could make you see anything and everything. She could even fashion the stars into a necklace and the moon into a crown."

I would have liked to allow her to reminisce a bit longer, but I needed to know one more thing. "Are you really an outlaw like the Keeper said?"

The smile left her face. "It's all a misunderstanding really."

"But your brother shouldn't have tried to take the pearl from you." I stooped and picked up a block of salt.

"Families are overrated things, boy." She busied herself by tilting her head to study the wound in her wing. "You ought to be glad you don't have one."

"Really?" I began to crumble the edges of the block. "People used to make me feel like it was my fault that I was an orphan."

She gave a bitter laugh before she licked the blood from the cut. "No, be grateful that you don't have a family. All the gossip. All the meddling. All the betrayals."

Back in Amity I had built up my own picture of family life, so it was hard to accept her portrait. "You expect that kind of behavior from enemies; but relatives are supposed to help you."

"Well, they don't," she replied crisply. "In fact, relatives will stab you in the back twice as fast and hard as an enemy." She spoke with conviction—as if she'd had vast amounts of experience with such treachery.

Up until then I hadn't thought anything could be worse than being an orphan; but I guess I was wrong. It's funny, but right at that moment I wouldn't have traded places with Shimmer—even if someone had offered me the entire world. It was hard not to belong to a family. But, I suppose, it must be even harder to have a family reject you—and worse, to make your entire race also turn their backs on you.

"I'm sorry," I murmured.

If she had been a cat, you would have seen the fur bristling around her neck. As it was, she clenched her teeth almost as if there was a deeper wound inside her than the one on her wing. "I don't want your pity."

I felt tremendously clumsy at the moment, unsure of how to handle my large, dangerous companion. At the same time, though, I felt a need to know the truth. "So capturing Civet means more than regaining the sea," I said, remembering the Keeper's words. "If you caught her, the other dragons would also have to forgive you."

She refused to look at me. "I told you. There's nothing to forgive. It's simply a matter of clearing up a misunderstanding."

I couldn't see any good in badgering her anymore. "Whatever you say." When I had enough salt, I dropped the block and shoved my way in between her head and her wounded wing. What she needed at the moment was kind acts more than words. "This salt should keep the cut from getting infected." I began to pat the salt onto the gash.

"Gently." She clenched her teeth at the sudden pain.

"I'm trying to do my best." When I had taken care of her other wounds as well, I stepped back and dusted off my hands. "Do you think you'll be able to fly now?"

She moved her wing timidly and grimaced. "No, it feels

even worse now. We're just going to have to walk to the city. Due west should do it."

"That won't be any picnic." Grimly I surveyed the dead landscape. There wasn't any sign of the Keeper or of anything else except for a long mound that was close to three meters high and seemed to stretch for kilometers on either of its two visible sides. "Are you sure this is your sea? It's all flat except for that heap."

"That's odd." Shimmer seemed puzzled. "I don't remember any natural feature like that." She looked all about. "Still, I have the funny feeling that I ought to know it." She tried to orient herself by glancing at the stars and then at the mountains we had just left. She plopped back on her belly as if someone had just kicked her. "No, it couldn't be." She began to check the surroundings again with growing desperation and then swung round to face the mound once more. "In my worst nightmares, I never dreamed things would be this bad." The salt crunched underneath her feet. "All the marvelous domes and spires are gone."

I studied the mound but I couldn't figure out from its present shape what it had once been. "What is it?"

"The glory of my clan." Two tears, each the size of my fist, suddenly rolled down her cheeks. The moisture made

*her scales gleam with little glints of metallic blue and gold.
"This mound used to be my grandfather's palace and it
was all of living coral. I knew the coral worms would die
with the sea gone; but I never expected this."*

*"The winds must have worn it down." Now that she
had told me what the mound had once been, I thought
I could make out hollows in the side where gates and
windows must have been at one time.*

*"I used to dream about coming back here." She shook
her head as if she still didn't want to believe her eyes. "Whenever things got bad or when I was stuck in filth and mire
up to my ankles, I would remember the palace."*

*"I wish I could have seen it," I said, trying to sympathize
with her.*

*Unfortunately, sympathetic words only seemed to make
her feel sadder. "It was best in the morning." She stared
up at the empty sky with a fierce longing. "The first stray
beams of daylight used to dance like long, thin snakes down
through the palace spires. And when I was small, I used
to float just above the palace and I would twist round and
round in the water, pretending that I was wrapping myself
in veils of light." She let out a low, heartfelt moan. "And
now it's as if the palace and the sea had never been."*

Though she was feeling pretty low, I thought I could at least encourage her. "Once we get back the sea, you can always rebuild it."

Lowering her head, she butted me away roughly. "Do you think just anyone can shape bunches of worms into spires? Even in my father's time, we could never repair things so that they were as good as they originally had been." Her wings drooped alarmingly and her whole body seemed to collapse—as if she were suddenly thousands of years older. "What's the use of trying?"

She rested her head between her forefeet. "When I first had to go into exile, I always used to comfort myself with the thought that eventually my clan would reconsider my sentence and pardon me. But then Civet came and scattered them. So instead I began to tell myself that once someone recovered the sea, the clan would need every dragon to help restore it and I would still be forgiven. But no one did. And finally in Amity, I started to hope that I could accomplish everything myself." She gave a bitter little laugh. "I was a fool."

At that moment she looked just like some dog that had received one too many beatings. With a start I realized that, as big and deadly as she was, she really needed me at that moment. I mean, without her hope and pride, she was as low as the mangiest cur in Amity. It made me want to protect her somehow from any more beatings. It was an odd feeling in a way, because before this, I had never had anyone to take care of.

I suspected, though, that hopeful words would only drive her deeper into despair. If I wanted to get her moving again, I was going to have to do it a different way. I stood over her and slowly planted a fist on either hip. "It's no good wallowing in self-pity. How do you know what your palace is going to look like? Maybe it'll be even better than the other one."

Shimmer stiffened ever so slightly, but I took it as a positive sign that she was getting back some of her old spirit. "My grandfather's palace was counted one of the great wonders of the dragon kingdoms. How can you improve upon that?"

"Why do you want to give up before you even try?" I demanded.

Shimmer's head rose. "We dragons," she declared with regal disdain, "do not turn our backs upon the past as you humans do."

It was good, in a way, that she was beginning to ham it up once again as a dragon princess. Impulsively, I grabbed her snout so that I could look her straight in the eye. "And maybe you dragons spend too much time reminiscing. Why does the future always have to be worse than the past?"

Shimmer's eyes almost crossed as they stared at the hands I had dared lay on her snout. She reared upward with all of her old righteous indignation—and lifted my feet off the ground. She made noises as if she would have liked to answer me but couldn't while I had hold of her.

"Don't just tell me that I'm wrong," I challenged her. "Show me. Build a palace, and if it isn't as good as your grandfather's, then I'll apologize."

She grabbed hold of my collar and snatched me away from her snout. When she had set me down on my feet, I waited for her to start raving. But though her eyebrows twitched angrily, she only opened her mouth and shut it several times as if rejecting several possible answers. And then, grudgingly, reluctantly, she broke into a smile. "Well," she admitted finally, "I like your attitude even if I don't quite agree with it."

"So let's get your sea." I pivoted, all set to charge off after Civet.

Almost affectionately, she caught hold of the seat of my

pants. *"You're going south, boy."* She nodded her head in a different direction. *"Due west is that way."*

"Oh," I said in a small voice. Rather sheepishly I adjusted my steps.

CHAPTER TEN

Thorn and I could make only very slow progress, since we had to pick our way across the seafloor. I walked bowlegged, with both pairs of feet half shuffling along. Even then, the salt would break into jagged cakes with edges that looked sharp enough to cut through even my tough hide. Puffs of fine white salt swirled around my legs, quickly coating my ankles until I seemed to be wearing white boots.

We quickly found that it was easier for Thorn if he adopted a course parallel to mine rather than following along behind me on the broken salt chunks that were left strewn in my wake. Even worse, the winds blew the salt into our faces. I felt it only as a slight stinging against my thick skin, but the salt must have driven into the boy's skin like dozens of needles.

"Are you all right, boy?" I asked him.

He was trying to hold his ragged collar shut. "I think the worst part of all this is the salt that gets under my clothes. It's awfully itchy."

I glanced behind us at the mountains. "It'll be daylight soon. We'll take a short rest and then push on. I think we should cover as much distance as we can while we're fresh and strong."

It was easier walking in the daytime because the winds died down then—though the salt flats reflected the sun so intensely that the world seemed to be swallowed up in a fiery light. Wherever I looked to the west, there was only the unending white plain. It made me feel small and insignificant—like some little ant who could crawl forever and never reach the edge. The boy was the only tiny little patch of color in all that whiteness, and even his outline appeared to waver in that white light.

The glare from the seafloor seemed to threaten the

sky itself. Near the horizon the sky was almost a milky-blue color, as if the whiteness of the seafloor were slowly mixing with heaven. Even directly overhead the sky seemed pale and washed out.

I did not let us make camp until the sun had set and neither of us could take another step. After a quick meal from Thorn's sack and long, lingering swallows of our water ration, we tried to lie down.

But even with my tough hide, it felt as if I were trying to sleep on a bed of rocks, because the salt crust had broken up into little lumps underneath me. As if that wasn't bad enough, an icy gale began to howl down from the mountains. I had never remembered the winds being this fierce or this cold, but I usually had kept at least ten meters of water screening me from their ugly touch.

I glanced at the boy. He huddled up with his arms wrapped around himself as if he could hold in all of his body warmth that way. He looked so helpless at that moment that I had to resist the urge to smooth the hair from his eyes. A dragon's claws are meant more for fighting than for showing affection. I had to remember that for all of his brave talk, he was a rather fragile little thing.

The wind blew even harder than before and the boy began to shiver. He would wake soon if this kept up. I found myself sliding sideways until my body was between the boy and the winds. For a moment I thought about expanding my size, but I decided that it was better for me to save as much of my strength as I could for our long trip.

Instead, I laid my head down, raising my one good wing so that the wind broke against it and my body rather than against the sleeping boy. His shivering stopped and his body began to relax. It wasn't too long before he began to snore—rather loudly, I might add, for a snout that small.

I pillowed my own head against a foreleg. And, as I lay drowsing, it almost seemed as if I could hear the distant sound of the surf breaking against the rocks. I told myself it was only the wind. But then, as my eyelids finally drooped heavily, I saw the breezes raise streamers of salt spray ten meters high. They drifted like ghostly seaweed all around us. And far overhead, in the light of the newly risen moon, two clouds floated majestically like ghostly whales. And I felt as if I were almost home.

I slept like that the entire night until the rising sun woke me. Raising my eyelids a crack, I saw that the boy was still asleep, so I crept carefully back to my old spot.

After all, there was no sense in spoiling the boy.

That second day was even harder than the first. The winds picked up until even my face felt as if it had been scoured with salt and my legs began to feel numb. If it was hard for me, it must have been even rougher for the boy, because he began to stumble with painful regularity.

I tried to encourage him by pointing to the faint black smudge on the horizon. "Those are the mountains that mark the western shore. It's not too far now."

But the mountains seemed to grow only a little closer that day and the next. Even worse, we entered into an area where the salt had formed into a hard, brittle crust that would sometimes break into slabs and then tilt upward on either side. As a result, we cut our hands or feet or legs on the knife-sharp edges of the slabs when we fell. And afterward the salt would cling maddeningly to the wounds. The salt even got into our noses and mouths, so that it was hard not to take a drink of water every few steps.

Even so, I thought talking might distract the boy's mind from our suffering. I described the large spacious parks that had surrounded the palace. Beds of sea anemones had opened like flowers, and sea lizards had sung while schools of fish danced overhead with long, veillike fins.

The boy would ask questions while we walked; but after a time he fell silent, merely grunting every now and then. Finally, when he started to stagger, I licked my dry, cracked lips. "You'd better let me carry the things."

"I can manage." His voice was high and thin from thirst—like the wind blowing over a dry, broken reed.

"It's not as if there were any dragons around to see me carrying them." I tried to pluck the bag and gourd away from him, but he held on to them grimly, insisting that he could manage. For a moment there was an absurd tug-of-war there in the middle of the seafloor. "I like your spirit," I said to him, "but not at this moment. GIVE me those things."

And he was so startled, he let go and almost fell as I slung the sack of food and water bag around my neck. "Come along now." But we had not gone two kilometers before I heard a loud crack behind me. I turned to see Thorn floundering in the spot where he had fallen in a small pile of salt chunks.

Thorn must have heard my exasperated snort, because he immediately called to me that he was coming. He struggled to his knees and tried to push himself up—but his arms began to shake and suddenly he collapsed on his face again.

I swung back to him. "We shouldn't try to rest until tonight." I stood over him for a moment. "We have to get off the seafloor before our supplies run out."

"I know." He didn't even have the energy to lift his head, but left his cheek and mouth pressed against the salt. "I'll be with you in a moment."

I prodded him with my forefoot. "We'll be out of here in two days if we can keep moving."

He fended off my paw with a feeble wave of his hand. "You go on without me then. I told you I'll catch up."

I shifted my feet uncertainly. "You said at the very

start that I could just leave you if you didn't keep up."

"And I'll show you that you were wrong about me." He frowned in annoyance. "I'll stick to you closer than your shadow—after I've taken a little nap."

I turned around but didn't take two steps before I glanced behind me. He was still lying sprawled on the blocks of salt. "I'm leaving," I warned him.

"I'll be right with you," he insisted drowsily.

I knew the little fool wasn't likely to get up once he fell asleep; but I had done what I could to keep him from coming along. It was not my responsibility. After all, I had warned him not to come. I took another step and paused, looking once again over my shoulder. He was a small, forlorn bundle of rags on the salt floor. "I'm really leaving this time."

He raised a weary hand and waved it. "I'll see you soon."

Facing forward resolutely, I began to lift my legs as I marched on. But I couldn't help thinking that the last few days had been very hard even on my dragon's constitution. He had really done quite well for a human.

On the other hand, I didn't see why I had to carry

the boy. It was one thing for me to share the burden of our supplies, but quite another to let him keep riding on top of me as if I were some camel.

And yet loyalty ought to count for something in this wicked world. I looked at the shimmering wasteland, remembering how it had been when the seafloor had been lush with life and the great dragons had floated so majestically overhead through the warm, languid water.

They had looked so beautiful and spoken so nobly, and yet when my mother had died, not one of my friends or servants would support me and testify about my mother's promise of the pearl. They had all been too frightened of my brother. And later, after I had fled, apparently not one of them had raised any objections when my brother had outlawed me. No dragon had served me half as well as the little human.

I sighed, deciding that I was becoming a sentimental fool; but I turned slowly and retraced my steps.

He was still lying there like some pathetic little doll. "Why do you have to prove that I'm wrong?" I demanded.

"Why do you have to insist that you're always right?" he countered.

We could have been out there arguing the whole day, so I simply squatted down on the salt. "Hop on," I sighed.

"What?" He raised a salt-covered cheek.

"I said to hop on." I glowered at him. "Just don't make a regular habit of this." He tried to shove himself up but he still didn't have the strength, so I finally had to grab him by the scruff of his neck and sling him over my back.

During the rest of the day he slept, and that evening I had to force him to eat and drink his portion. When he was asleep, I crawled between him and the cold winds. I fell asleep to memories of soft sunlight trailing like veils of lace through the water.

CHAPTER ELEVEN

When I tried to open my eyes the next morning, I felt as if someone had flung hot sand against them. With a groan, I immediately shut them again.

I could hear the boy stir and wake up. "How long have you been sleeping like that?" Thorn asked. Too late, I remembered that I was still in my position as a wind barrier.

I tried to speak, but my throat was so dry that I could only make croaking sounds at first. I managed to swallow after some difficulty. "Never mind that."

I probed gently at my eyelids. They felt puffy and swollen. "Something's wrong with my eyes." I tried to open them again but it was too painful.

I heard several small snaps as he came closer to me to study my face. "A traveler to the inn," said the boy, "once told us that people who live in the northern mountains sometimes become temporarily blind because of all the white snow. The sun reflects off it, you see, and burns their eyes. Or something like that. A day of rest usually cures it. I guess the sun shines off the white salt just like to does off snow."

"We don't have enough food to wait a day." I rose grimly and tried to walk, but could manage only a cautious shuffle before I tripped and fell. My head broke the salt into small sharp knifelike chunks that cut my chin.

The boy clumsily plodded up to me as I lay there. "Are you all right?" He patted my shoulder.

"I'm cold and hungry and thirsty and now I'm blind." I curled up my lip sarcastically. "What do you think?"

The boy was quiet, and that automatically made me wonder since he was usually such a chatty little thing. Suddenly he edged in closer. "I've got an idea," the boy said. "If you shrank down to the size of a cat, I could carry you."

I gave a snort and clapped a forefoot crunchingly against the salt. "Don't be ridiculous."

"But I feel fine after a day's rest." The salt snapped underneath him as he sat down beside me.

"That's not the problem at all." I raised my head up high enough to shake it. "It just wouldn't do for a princess to be smaller than you."

A dragon would have politely let the matter rest at that point; but Thorn, with the rudeness typical of his kind, kept on. "But you're not really a princess, you're an outlaw."

"I still haven't sunk that low," I snapped.

His voice took on a worried note. "I'm afraid you're going to hurt yourself stumbling around. You could even break a leg."

I hadn't had anyone fuss over me like this even when I had lived as a princess among other dragons. We dragons pride ourselves on our robust health. Even a sniffly snout could be a source of great embarrassment. "I'll keep up with you even if I have to inch along on my belly."

His voice grew high and sweet—like someone trying to coax a stubborn child. "But you said yesterday that no one would see us—so who would know?"

"*I* would know," I said in my iciest voice, "and so would you."

"Honestly." The boy pounded his fist against what I suppose was a salt block. "Why do you always have to stand on your silly pride?"

I was so irritated with him that I spoke without thinking. "Because it's all that I've had sometimes."

"I see," the boy said in a small voice, and added sympathetically, "I suppose it hasn't been all that easy being an outlaw."

I squirmed, unable to recall a time when anyone had wanted to hear of my exile. "No." I exhaled slowly. "It hasn't been."

"Well, what does it take to convince you that I'm your friend?" The boy sounded genuinely puzzled.

I scratched my forehead, feeling just as bewildered as he was. "I don't know," I had to confess. "It's been centuries since the situation last came up."

"I'm not in the least bit surprised," he said drily.

"No one's asking you to stay." I reared my head up angrily. "I don't need you or anyone. I decided long ago after the 'misunderstanding' that I'd never depend on anyone to help me."

"No, of course not," he was quick to agree. Even though he was young, years of working in Knobby's inn had taught him how to soothe people. "I was just trying to repay you for carrying me yesterday."

That, of course, put a slightly different light on things. I considered the matter from a number of angles. When you came right down to it, I didn't exactly enjoy the prospect of tripping all day long. I nodded my head finally. "I guess it really wouldn't be like I owed you a favor, would it?"

"Oh, no," the boy reassured me hastily. "I'd just be paying off a few of my debts to you."

I swung my head in the direction of his voice. "And you wouldn't tell any other humans?"

"I swear."

Even though it hurt, I raised one eyelid to make sure he was holding up his right hand. When I saw that he was, I closed my eye again. The humiliation was almost more than I could bear, and yet he did make sense. I wriggled my snout. "All right," I said reluctantly, "but on your back, mind you, not in front like some pet puppy."

"Whatever you say," he agreed, and I heard the sound of cloth tearing.

"What are you doing now?" I demanded irritably.

"I'm going to tear a strip from my shirt and cut slits for my eyes," he explained. "When I tie it around my head, the black cloth should keep me from going blind." He added, "I hope."

After touching the pearl, I drew a sign in the air with my claw and murmured a spell under my breath. Shrinking is always more painful than growing, since for a moment all your bones jam together like a crowd on market day; but the pain was over quickly enough as I became the size of a cat.

I couldn't help squirming though when he picked me up and laid me across his shoulders. "You're an awfully bony little thing, aren't you?" I complained.

"Ow. Don't dig your claws in." He wriggled his shoulders so violently that I felt as if I were caught in a tremendous earthquake.

I will say, though, that a day's rest seemed to have done him enormous good, since he marched along steadily and by that evening had taken us to the western edge of the sea. However, I would not let him stop there where, he said, the ground was pink with a mixture of white salt and the red, clayish soil blown down from the foothills.

Instead, I made him walk on until we were actually in the hills, which were still covered by a thick forest of dead trees and tangled, leafless scrub. Even so, it took him a while before he had a good fire going. I was still feeling a little too tired and sick to take my proper size, so after we had shared the last of our provisions, I simply curled up with my face turned toward the cheerful fire.

I have heard stories concerning the dragons of other worlds who could actually breathe fire. I had always thought it would be inconvenient whenever a dragon wanted to take a swim. Wouldn't she turn the surrounding water into steam? But at the moment I had to admit that it would have been rather quicker than to have the boy fuss with that awkward knife and flint of his.

"How are your eyes?" Thorn asked.

I blinked them experimentally. "They only ache a little bit now. I should be fine by tomorrow."

He cleared his throat. "I don't mind carrying you."

"No, I'll be able to walk on my own." I wrapped my tail around myself.

He cleared his throat again. "But I like being *useful.*" He emphasized the last word meaningfully.

I suppose I had made a slight miscalculation when I once had called him useless—so I did owe him some sort of apology. "Yes, well," I murmured drowsily, "you've done surprisingly well."

"Aren't you even going to thank me?" he protested.

I sighed. Give humans a spoonful of flattery and they expect the entire bottle. Well, he was playing that game with the wrong person. I've never been one to spoil people with too many pretty words.

"Why should I thank you?" I asked. "If you think about the situation, you'll realize that I was just shading the back of your head against the sun. In fact, I probably saved your life by keeping you from getting sunstroke. However"—I sniffed my most regal sniff—"you don't find *me* fishing for compliments."

The boy sat in stunned silence for a long time— in fact he was quiet so long that I almost opened my eyes to check on him. But he finally burst out laughing. "You're impossible."

I corrected him proudly. "*Unique* is a better word." And I drifted off to sleep.

The next morning my eyes were almost as good

as new. I wished I could have said the same thing about my wing, which, though it was healing nicely, was still not strong enough for flying. So I examined the soles of my feet instead. "Well," I sighed, "at least these are holding up all right."

I was just about to resume my usual size when several pebbles suddenly fell down the hillside. The boy jumped back, but I crouched staring up the slope. "Well, fancy that." I narrowed my eyes. "There must be something still living up there."

Telling the boy to start another fire, I shot up the slope to begin my hunt. It took me about an hour, but I came trotting back with a half dozen olive-skinned lizards dangling by their tails from my mouth.

Thorn took out his knife and began to clean them. "Maybe you've discovered a new vocation."

"Quiet," I warned him, "or I might make myself as big as a mountain and have you for a snack as well." But to my annoyance, he did not seem in the least bit frightened. In fact, I seemed to amuse him—just as an elderly, eccentric aunt might have.

When we had finished our breakfast, I grew to the correct length and led him along the hills.

"Let's see. There used to be a river that formed

part of the human route from River Glen." My eyes searched the hills ahead of us.

"Humans used to come here?" the boy asked.

"All the time." I picked my way through the dirt. "In fact, it was the trade with my clan that made River Glen so prosperous. Some people even called that city the dragons' market."

Eventually we found the steep-sided canyon through which fresh mountain water had once flowed, though the river, like the sea it had once fed, had long since vanished; but the floor of the canyon was fairly easy traveling. We even managed to find a small puddle of brackish water—left from some rain, I guess. We had no choice but to fill our gourd with it.

That night we made camp halfway up one side of the river canyon on a wide, spacious ledge partitioned by crumbling walls. The ledge had once been the lowest of a series of terraces my father had ordered created. They had once reached all the way to the very top of the canyon. We sprawled on hard dirt where the outline of some vineyard's shriveled grape vines could still be seen. All around us, dead fruit trees rose like ghostly hands.

I caught several more lizards while Thorn made a fire from the branches of the surrounding trees. Their wood gave off the scent of the long-vanished orchards. "At almost any time of the year," I reminisced, "the air would be filled with the smell of pomegranates and pears, plums and dates and almonds—and the terraces would be white with blossoms."

Thorn stared into the fire for a moment as if he could see the scene I was describing. "And then came Civet?"

I gave a quick, curt nod of my head. "And then came Civet."

"But why did she steal your sea?" Thorn wanted to know.

"Well," I said, after considering the matter, "the Keeper said that she had once lived in River Glen— I never knew that. Perhaps something happened to her there that made her hate the place. If that's so, it wouldn't take much to hate my clan as well. After all, we were the source of the city's wealth." I shoved another piece of wood into the fire. The dry wood seemed to explode into flame. "We won't really know until we catch her, I suppose."

Thorn's hands cradled his chin and he murmured

dreamily. "It'll be nice when the river starts flowing again."

"Perhaps you can even have a little estate along here." I picked up a fat lizard that I had marked for myself and stuck it on a wooden branch. "But 'first things first,' as my mother always used to say." I began to roast the lizard. "Let's catch Civet."

CHAPTER TWELVE

It took us another day to journey up the canyon; but eventually we reached a circular basin of crumbly red rock that had once been a large lake—the source of the river. A dozen wide stairways ended a quarter of the way down one side of the basin.

I pointed a claw to several ledges where there used to be wharves for all the riverboats. "This was always a favorite spot for travelers. You would stop here and rest after the journey over the mountain pass." Then I swept a foreleg to indicate all the stairways. "My father ordered his craftsmen to carve the various streambeds into steps, and then used his magic to make the water sing as it slipped along the stones."

Thorn wiped the sweat from his forehead. "Now all that's left is the heat rising from the stones."

I had to agree that it was quite a contrast from the old days, when we dragons used to gather at the foot of the falls to hear the music of the water and feel the spray rise and perhaps tumble about in the eddies and currents beneath the falls. By scrambling up the gradual slope at one side of the bay, I managed to get us onto the old road that would take us through a mountain pass to River Glen itself.

At times we could trace the original stones that had once been part of the road, but avalanches and earth tremors as well as the weather itself had slowly ruined the road until it was little more than a narrow track.

Halfway into the mountains, I tried my wings again and found that the wound had healed well enough for me to make a quick pounce on a mountain goat. So with plenty of food, and water from various springs we found en route, we were feeling much stronger by the end of the third day when we topped the mountain pass.

Below us lay a large, oval valley formed by two spurs of the mountain range. A small river fell down the northern spur, slipping along the center of the valley and through the narrow gap between the two spurs to join the great Arrow River beyond. It had been a nice little valley once, but centuries of cutting the trees had gullied the surrounding mountains and hillsides. Mining and quarrying had only worsened the situation, filling the valley floor with huge hills of black sludge, and the river itself was filthy from the surrounding factories on the banks. Though there were a few fields being cultivated, most of the ground was dry and barren.

Over on the right bank was a city of pink stone with broad, spacious streets and houses whose walls were decorated with sea scenes or carved like coral reefs. The sight made me feel a bit homesick, since the city folk had tried to copy some of the things they had seen among the dragons.

However, time had not been kind to River Glen. The roofs of several buildings had collapsed, and many streets were filled with dirt and dust.

"Has Civet been here already?" Thorn wondered. "It looks like it's half ruined already."

"It's not the way I remember it, but I think that's because people have been leaving after the trade with my clan was cut off." But after studying the scene for a moment, I decided against flying in. My wings were certainly strong enough now, but I couldn't be sure she wasn't there ahead of us and simply waiting for the right time to strike. Instead, I changed myself into a richly robed merchant and Thorn into my servant.

After resting a bit, I led the way down the trail. "As I recall, there used to be a very nice inn by the gate, with fat meat dumplings." I added, "If it's still there."

The towers on either side of the city gate were filled with crossbowmen, while groups of men of various skin and hair colors stood at attention with long spears on both sides of the road. A small, yellow-bearded officer strutted back and forth between the two lines.

He wore large, blue silk trousers tucked into his red boots and a tiger skin draped around his chest. His only armor was an iron helmet with a spike on top from which silk ribbons flew. He held up a hand when he saw us. "Identify yourselves and state your business in the city of River Glen."

I sniffed him suspiciously but he didn't have Civet's scent—or any human scent for that matter. He smelled like hot, dusty stones on a dry summer's afternoon. "Who or what are you?" I demanded.

The officer raised his hand and the men behind him immediately pointed their weapons at us. "We were sent here by that magnificent hero, the Great Sage Equal to Heaven."

Great Sage indeed! It was a fancy title for a vain, thieving troublemaker more widely known as Monkey. I'm ashamed to say that even the dragons weren't able to stop him when Monkey forced my uncle, the King of the Golden Sea, to give him a magical iron rod that could grow from the size of a toothpick to a pole some two meters long. Wielding that fearsome magical weapon and backed by an army of monsters, he had tried to set up his own kingdom.

Fortunately for the world, he had met his match in a kindly wizard called the Old Boy (he was called that because he had been born with white hair). After a long, hard-fought battle, the Old Boy had finally managed to place a gold circlet around Monkey's head that caused him great pain whenever he disobeyed. The ape supposedly served the Old Boy now, atoning for his past sins by helping his master in various good works. But from what I had heard, the unruly Monkey sometimes got carried away in helping someone— rather like the person who uses a mallet to swat the mosquito on your nose.

I studied the officer thoughtfully. The tales said that Monkey had been born from a stone egg, which might account for this particular creature's odd scent. "You wouldn't happen to be that very same ape, would you?"

"Not so loud." Monkey made hushing noises. "The Old Boy ordered me to protect River Glen from Civet. That's why I'm in disguise."

I smiled wryly. "It's hardly a disguise when you boast about yourself."

Monkey glared at me. "I am the Master of the Seventy-two Transformations," he protested. "I've probably forgotten more magic than you'll ever know." Suddenly he squinted at me. "Even if you may be of the dragonish persuasion." Monkey snorted. "Dragons were always deadliest with their tongues."

I drew myself up to my full human height. "Kindly show a little more respect. We dragons came into this world first."

Monkey folded his arms. "And never stop bragging about the fact until everyone is bored to tears."

I pursed my mouth. "My, what sharp little fangs we have. How would you like me to stamp on you like the vicious little worm you really are?"

Monkey's beard almost bristled in indignation. "I'd like to see you try."

Thorn pushed in suddenly between us. "Couldn't we carry on this discussion inside?" He looked back and forth between us significantly. "Where no one can overhear us?"

Monkey pointed at me as he stepped forward. "It was this overgrown lizard who started it all by assassinating my character."

"Your reputation was dead long ago." I leaned forward against Thorn. "In fact, it's rather overripe— if not outright rotten."

Thorn tried to shove the two of us apart. "Why don't the two of you send up fireworks and paint signs telling Civet who you are."

Monkey stepped back, giving a hitch to his trousers.

"What about postponing this argument?"

"A contest of magic then," I suggested, "after we've caught Civet."

Monkey looked at me strangely. "Let's discuss that, shall we?" He pivoted on his heel and beckoned for us to follow him. I couldn't help noticing, though, as we passed between the two lines of spearsmen, that they all looked like Monkey—even if their skins were of different colors, including blue skins and green hair.

He led us into a small but comfortable room within the base of the left tower and ordered food and tea to be brought to us.

I couldn't help squirming as I tried to scratch my back. "Confound this human shape. It always itches so."

Thorn set our things down in a corner. "The shutters are closed. Why don't you take your true shape?"

"Well, it would feel better." I wriggled almost as if someone had dropped an entire jar of fleas down my back. Turning away from Monkey so that he could not see the magical sign or even read my lips as I mouthed the spell, I changed myself back into a dragon.

"Oof. Have a care," Monkey said angrily as my lovely dragon shape filled the tiny room, overturning a table and pressing Monkey himself against a wall. He kicked at my tail. "Can't you shrink a bit?"

I raised my wings, twisting my head around so I could look at Monkey over my shoulder. "A dragon princess must always be of a suitable length."

"Then," Monkey grumbled, "we're going to have to use your stomach for a tabletop, because there's no room to set up the regular one."

I sighed. "Very well, if I have no choice." Again careful to hide the sign and spell from Monkey, I shrank down to something a little over two meters long.

"Just to show you that I mean to be honest," Monkey said, "I'll take my own shape." He muttered a spell, and with a shiver he shouted, "Change." His head, neck and hands were covered with shaggy yellow hair and he was wearing a coarse gray robe with a tiger skin that had been fastened on his shoulder so that it hung in front of his robe. On his head was some funny floppy cap of shiny silk.

I pointed to his hairless tail. "What happened to you?"

He jerked a thumb outside. "I talked all the inhabitants into leaving so I could set up an ambush for
Civet. Once they were gone, I used my magic to
change the hairs of my tail into people." He tilted
his head up smugly. "Clever, isn't it?"

"How did you ever manage to convince the original
people to leave?" I wondered.

"I can be very persuasive." He whipped his bald
tail back and forth proudly.

"Humph," I snorted. "You mean you bullied them
into leaving. I doubt if that's what your master actually
had in mind when he sent you here."

He lowered his tail. "I don't want to be stuck here
forever. I intend to catch her and stop her mischief
once and for all."

"Are you sure she doesn't know about your trap?"
I asked.

"Yes." He took off his cap and twirled it on his
finger. There was a slender gold circlet around his
head. "When Monkey plans an ambush, he does it
thoroughly. I sent out hundreds of scouts to make
sure we weren't observed. So you needn't worry,
Lady . . . ?"

"I use the name of Shimmer," I said, and presented

my back for Thorn to scratch. "Of the clan of the Lost Sea."

"Oh, you're *that* dragon." Monkey cupped his paw around his chin thoughtfully. "And who's the boy?"

"My name is Thorn," the boy said. "I don't know who my family is."

Monkey studied his face intently. "I'm sure I've seen your face before, boy."

Thorn stopped scratching me. "Where?" he asked eagerly.

Monkey studied the boy and then wrinkled his nose. "Give me a moment and I'll remember."

The boy slumped against a wall. "I was hoping you could tell me if I had a family."

Monkey held up a paw. "Just give me a moment and I'll remember."

I didn't want him to disappoint the boy any further. "Admit it," I scolded Monkey. "You're just getting too old."

Monkey rocked back on his haunches. "Ask me any one of the hundred dragon kings and queens and I'll tell you not only their names, but the names of all their children, uncles, aunts, and even cousins to the thirty-second degree."

At that moment one of Monkey's counterfeit people brought a large tray inside. There was a platter heaped with various meat pastries as well as teacups and a pot of tea. While the counterfeit person poured the tea, I couldn't help glaring at Monkey. "I'm glad to see that your tongue hasn't worn out even if your memory might have."

Monkey picked up a cup of tea. "Cheers," he said and leaned his head back as if he were drinking.

Reassured and feeling thirsty, I downed a cup of tea myself and poured another. The boy, however, only sipped from his as if Monkey's words had made him lose all interest in eating and drinking.

"You have to keep your strength up," I told the boy, and put a dumpling on a plate in front of him.

Thorn stretched and yawned. "I think I'd prefer to rest."

I couldn't help copying him. "I don't know what's gotten into me." I covered my mouth with my paw.

Thorn dropped his arms sleepily. "We've had a long, hard trip."

"There's a pallet right over there." Monkey pointed.

But Thorn didn't even make it there. "Right," he

said and fell backward with a thud to begin sleeping exactly where he had fallen on the floor.

Monkey set his cup of tea down. I saw it was still almost full. "You only pretended to drink." I glared at him accusingly.

"This is *my* ambush," Monkey warned me. "I told my master that I'd save the city and capture Civet and I will. I'm not having you charge in at the last moment and claim all the glory."

I tried to raise a foot to slash at him, but my foot felt as if it were made of stone. "I just want Civet's pebble, you fool ape."

"And you can have it"—Monkey shoved my shoulder with his paw—"but after *I* have her in chains."

I tried to move my lips to warn him about the mist stone, but my lips would not respond. I could only topple backward, my mind slipping into the darkness before my head even touched the floor.

CHAPTER THIRTEEN

I could not have said whether I slept days or only hours when Thorn finally tried to wake me. I could feel him poking at my shoulder and hear his voice calling me—as if from a great distance. But I found it impossible to even open my eyes.

It was as if I were down a deep well, so that by the time the sounds drifted down through the water, they were rather thin and garbled.

But it seemed to me as if I could hear Monkey call, "And where are you going, old woman?"

An elderly woman's voice creaked like wood so old that it was going to crack at any moment. "I'm bringing water for my master. He must have fresh water when he mixes his ink."

It had to be Civet, since only she would pretend to know someone in the evacuated city.

"He's a rather fussy master." The fool ape, I suppose, wanted to show off a bit more before making the arrest.

"He's a great writer," she replied. "And very impatient. Now let me pass."

"I'm rather thirsty, old woman," Monkey said casually. "What about a sip?"

"My master needs the water," she insisted.

"Wake up," Thorn urged me. "I think it's Civet."

"Two buckets?" Monkey taunted. "He couldn't need that much water even if he wrote with both hands."

"Hurry," Thorn said to me urgently.

I felt almost as if my eyelids were made of lead when I tried to raise them. Outside I could hear the sound of splashing and loud gulping.

"No, no," the old woman called out in alarm. "You said you'd just take a sip, not the whole bucket."

"My sips," Monkey explained, "are other people's drinks." There was a clunk, as if he was throwing an empty wooden bucket to the side. "And my thirst is like no one else's."

It seemed to take an eternity for me to open my eyes. The light, slipping around the edges of the shuttered window, was a deep golden color—as if the sun were either just setting or rising.

Thorn was crouched by the windowsill peeping through the gap between the sill and the shutters. He waved his hand at me. "Hurry."

I could hear more swallowing noises while the old woman let out a wail. "Now I'll have to go back and get more water."

I craned my head over Thorn's shoulder to see Monkey standing in front of a bent little old woman. The front of Monkey's shirt was drenched with water and he was just in the process of turning the bucket over to show that it was completely empty.

"I've never had a better drink from such a lovely creature." He tossed the bucket to one side. "What was in the buckets? Poison for the city's wells?"

The old woman slowly straightened up. "You're a fool to drink it."

Hurriedly I tried to open the shutters but found they were locked.

Monkey sounded very pleased with himself as he began to boast in his usual way. "My magic's too strong to let me be killed. My enemies once tried to burn me alive in the hottest furnace in the world and didn't even singe one hair."

"You stupid ape." I tried to work the lock on the shutters, but there must have been some magic spell on it, because it wouldn't open. I dropped my head to peek at Monkey.

He was skipping about in a celebration dance. "You might have fooled all the dragons in the world, but you can't fool Monkey. I've been playing with you all this time."

I gritted my teeth and strained at the shutters. Cracks appeared in the plaster around the hinges, and the lock began to groan.

"Oh?" The old woman's voice was suddenly younger—like the voice of the Widow at the inn. "Actually, I would have said it was the other way around."

Down below, the old woman had reached into a pocket of her coat and pulled out the blue pebble. I couldn't understand what Civet was going to use it for. If she had wanted to escape, she had the mist stone. But then a new and horrible thought occurred to me. Could she hate the city enough to use the blue pebble to destroy it? Perhaps she had even stolen our sea for that very purpose. I began tugging with all my might at the shutters.

Monkey was going on in a high, pompous voice. "In the name of my master, the Old Boy, I arrest you for crimes against the people of this city and the dragons of the Lost Sea." And he ordered his guards to arrest her.

"Don't start counting the charges until I'm finished." Civet gave a loud, defiant laugh.

With one final heave, I ripped the shutters away from the window frame and threw them to the side. I was just climbing onto the sill when Civet tossed the pebble into the air. It arched upward, growing larger as it did so. First it was the size of a fist, then it was the size of a small pumpkin. Monkey made a leap at it, but he was off balance and taken by surprise, so that he merely tipped it behind him. By the time it arched downward, it had swollen so much that it was as large as a cart. When it crashed against the ground, the entire tower trembled. And there was a series of almost musical clinks—as if someone were smashing pieces of fine china in time to music.

A huge wall of water swept into the city through the gate. Monkey turned, his mouth opening in astonishment, as a sudden river of water washed him backward. He vanished instantly underneath the waves—much to the amusement of the old woman. Laughing, she raised her arms as if embracing the waters that flowed over her.

"She's loosed the entire sea," I gasped, stunned at the enormity of what she had done. Like Monkey, I had thought she would play some trick such as poisoning the city's wells. I had never dreamed that she would willingly destroy the pebble, because so much of her magic had been used to bind the sea into that stone. Throwing it away meant destroying a good deal of her own magic as well. She must truly have hated the city.

"The water keeps rising," Thorn said, and jumped back as the cold seawater surged over the windowsill. As if under deep pressure, more water sprayed from around the door to the room.

I turned to the boy in alarm. "Hold on to—" Suddenly a wave washed us away from the window. I lunged forward desperately and managed to grab a piece of his sleeve; but right at that moment the great iron hinges of the door gave way with a shriek. The heavy wooden door slammed against my foreleg so that I let go of the boy; and a sudden jet of water threw me back against the rear wall.

For a moment I couldn't see anything as the water foamed and churned about me. Finally, I had the good sense to duck my head beneath the surface of the water. Caught in the strong currents, chairs and cabinets whirled round and round like strangely shaped autumn leaves swept up by a wind. And then I saw the boy, his cheeks puffed out, his legs and arms making vague motions as if he were trying to swim. But what could he do with his feeble muscles against that flood?

Outside the tower, I knew, Civet was at her weakest. Not only was she in the wrong shape, but she would have few spells left to use.

But in order to catch her, I would have to let the boy drown. I couldn't let that happen after everything we had been through together.

With a strong, determined kick of my hindlegs and a sinuous twist of my body, I shot forward to catch him up in my forelegs. Churning the water with my hindlegs, I forced my way against the strong currents to the stairwell outside the room. I shifted him slightly so that I could grip his collar between my teeth. Then, half swimming and half crawling, I made my way up the steps to the next landing and found it was already almost filled with water.

At first I wasn't sure if the boy was breathing at all, so when I reached the next landing, I gave him a sharp rap on his back and the blow got him coughing again. With the boy dangling in front of me like a soggy kitten, I raced up the long flights of steps until I reached the very top of the tower.

It was full of soaked, tawny-colored monkeys about a half meter in height—I suppose they had changed to a more useful shape. There were hundreds more somersaulting into the sky as if they were moving up invisible steps cut into the air to join the others on the tower. But I thought they smelled rather like wet dogs.

"Let me through," I grumbled irritably through a mouthful of damp collar. I kicked and cuffed the crowd of little apes until I was right by the tower ramparts.

It was worse than I had feared. An entire sea covered the valley, though a small horde of apes was busy using boulders to dam the space between the mountain spurs to hold the sea back. Of the entire city, only the tops of the gate's towers showed above the water, which continued to rise.

"What's that?" Thorn leaned his belly against the rampart and pointed down below.

I swatted a somersaulting ape away from my face and looked over the edge. In the sea five meters beneath us were two murky shadows struggling toward the surface. Suddenly the wet head of the old woman bobbed up out of the water. She tried to leap into the air, but a slick Monkey pulled her back. They twisted and churned in the water, but neither one seemed to be gaining any advantage. It seemed as if they could have gone on wrestling that way for days.

Monkey must have been thinking along the same lines as I was, because he suddenly let her go and snatched what looked like a long needle from behind his ear.

"The idiot never gave me the time to tell him about the mist stone." Hurriedly I changed myself into my proper size.

"What are you doing?" Thorn demanded.

I shoved him back with my tail. "If I can't save the sea, I can at least take my revenge." Filled with a cold, bitter rage, I climbed onto the top of the rampart.

Beneath me, Monkey had already changed the needle into a rod of black iron with a golden loop at either end. It was a deadly weapon against everyone but the wearer of the mist stone, because she could change herself into a nebulous cloud.

Folding my wings in against my body and raising my forelegs over my head, I screamed my clan's battle cry and sprang toward the water.

But at the very instant that I leaped, the woman began to grow transparent. And then even her outline began to shimmer with little rainbow glints as the sunlight fell through her.

"N-O-O-O," I shouted in sheer frustration. I spread my wings with a great deal of effort and began to beat them frantically, trying to break my fall. The wind from my wings sent up great sheets of spray, and huge circles went rippling outward over the sea.

"You can't catch me now," the woman cried with almost childish delight—like some village girl who had won a footrace rather than a dreadful sorceress who had just flooded an entire city.

A silver mist, bound in tiny, ribbon-thin rainbows, rose from the water. It was in the general shape of a woman with long hair waving behind her. The only thing solid in the mist was a large, oval-shaped jewel which hung about her throat. It must be the Keeper's precious mist stone. I suppose she had kept it hidden underneath her blouse.

There was still a chance of capturing her if I could just get the magical gem. I lunged recklessly, but my claws just missed, ripping away a stray tendril of mist instead of the mist stone. Even as she rose, taking the jewel beyond my reach, the little wisp of mist sealed itself back to her vaporous body.

She seemed to be accelerating as she rose through the air. I beat my wings, determined to fly harder and faster than I ever had in my life until I caught up with her.

But below us, Monkey spluttered out, "Help me."

Instantly, the little monkeys on the towers and in the air began to leap toward the sea. They rained down like sleek, furry raindrops. Unfortunately, they fell right through the misty Civet and collided with me instead. My body jerked to a halt in the air as each monkey struck me like a small boulder. And then I was tumbling downward, caught up within a huge cloud of monkeys. We did not stop until we splashed thunderously through the sea all the way to the submerged streets.

By the time I was airborne again, Civet was already shooting like a rocket toward the northeast, where the Weeping Mountain lay. I beat my wings as hard as I could, straining every muscle; but I might just as well have been a snail trying to outhop a frog. Helplessly, I watched her vanish into the sky.

CHAPTER FOURTEEN

Below me, the waters of my old home looked so pretty and so pleasant. The sunlight slivered over the water's surface, shattering into a thousand miniature bows of light being pulled back by invisible archers. And each of them was sending an arrow into my soul.

And beneath the broken light, the sea was so blue—so much bluer than any sky I had ever seen. And so lifeless, for it's all the little living things that make a sea green. And this sea was dead—achingly, mockingly dead. And so, it seemed, were my dreams and hopes.

From underneath the shining, lifeless waters, the bells of the city began to ring—muffled and distorted as if they were wrapped in layer after layer of silk. No human hand rang them. It was the ghostly currents of the sea. It was almost as if the drowned city were mourning for itself and for my clan.

What good was I? None at all. I had failed not only to regain my sea, but even to take a nip from my enemy. The entire sky seemed to rest upon my back, and my wingbeats felt clumsy and weak. I couldn't help thinking that my clan might have been right to outlaw me because I was such a miserable failure as a dragon.

I lifted my head to look at the spot in the sky where Civet had disappeared. And I knew that if I was to keep my self-respect, I would have to follow her.

But I owed an explanation to the boy. I found him standing on the rampart of the tower where I had left him. The sea level had stopped rising about a meter from its top, so he was safe enough. But he looked like a bony rat who was shivering from his cold soaking. "Maybe I can warm you a bit before

I leave for Civet's mountain." I lowered myself around him, perching awkwardly on the rampart stones.

The boy rested his arms along my spine. "But you said no dragon's ever come out alive."

"Civet should be weaker now after working all that magic." I tried to dismiss the danger with a shrug.

"But there must be other possibilities," the boy said anxiously. "Why can't you settle here?"

"Because I have to resettle the original inhabitants back here," said a rather soggy Monkey, who somersaulted toward us, the iron rod still in one hand. "All I have to do is figure out how to get rid of this sea."

I was going to say something angry, but the boy spoke up before I could. He seemed determined to find alternatives to following Civet into her mountain. "Maybe the Old Boy could put the water back where it used to be."

"My master might be able to"—Monkey squatted in the air as if on an invisible cushion—"if I knew where to find him. But this is a deeply troubled world with so many injustices. Who knows where he is at the moment? I was simply to wait here and protect River Glen until he came for me or sent new commands." He murmured a word to the rod and it shrank instantly back to the size of a needle. "It'd be faster if I got Baldy's cauldron. Do you know where it is?"

"Who's Baldy?" the boy wanted to know.

"He was a creature who wanted to marry the daughter of the High King." Monkey held out the palm of his paw, and the little monkeys slowly began to spiral downward in a funnel-shaped cloud. Faster and faster they whirled, until their bodies began to blur into narrow lines that I realized were short hairs. "He used the magic cauldron to boil away the ocean until the High King gave in."

"The High King is my uncle," I said. "And I know for a fact that he made Baldy give him the cauldron in return."

"Oh." Monkey glanced behind him, watching critically as the hairs began to coat his tail again. "I suppose I'll just have to take Baldy's cauldron the way I took my magic rod."

I wrinkled my snout. "I've heard how you terrorized the King of the Golden Sea until he let you take the rod." I shook my claw at him. "But the High King is a different proposition from the King of the Golden Sea. The High King has vast armies that could stop even a magical ape. And even if you could get past them, the cauldron's in his deepest vaults and protected by all sorts of spells and magical creatures."

Monkey twitched his tail, which was now completely covered with fur. "Then I'll just have to sneak into the dragon kingdoms and steal it." He turned around to face us again as he puffed out his chest. "The moon sliding through the night sky makes more noise than I do."

"Why don't you help Shimmer catch Civet?" the boy suggested. "Maybe Civet could work some magic to take the sea away from here."

Monkey shook his head violently. "Even as weak as Civet may be after all this magic, I'd sooner jump into a pit of vipers than follow Civet into her mountain. My chances are far better going into the dragon kingdoms."

"Really?" The boy gave me a worried look.

"Yes, and she knows it too." Monkey glanced at me. "But dragons love feuding more than life itself."

"You'll be passing by some cities on your way there." I jerked a claw at Thorn. "So why don't you drop the boy off with his own kind?"

"Wait." The boy slapped his hand down hard on my hide. "I'm not finished with Civet yet."

I twisted my neck around to look at him. "Listen to me, boy. We've had our little adventure together; but it's time for us to go our separate ways. As much as I hate to agree with the ape, the odds still really aren't very good."

"And what were the odds when we met the Keeper or landed on the salt flats?" he reminded me stubbornly. "You're not nearly as clever as you think."

Monkey rested his paws on his knees. "Boy," he said urgently, "it's all very well to be loyal, but it's crazy to talk about going with her."

However, both Thorn and I ignored the ape. "It's been a long time since anyone's spoken to me like that," I said, and then added quietly, "and even longer since anyone meant it as I think you do." I tapped my claws on the rampart stones in a slow, thoughtful rhythm. "It's a little like hearing a pleasant song you used to sing long ago—a song that you thought everyone, including yourself, had forgotten."

Monkey drifted through the air until he was right next to us. He looked first at Thorn and then at me. "You can't be serious about taking the boy."

Thorn patted my side. "We're a team—whether she admits it or not."

"I don't know if I would go that far"—I sniffed—"but you do come in handy at times."

"I took off the gourd and the sack when we first went inside the tower," he said apologetically. "So I guess they're lost."

I gave him a lift up to his perch on the back of my neck. "Then we'll have our next meal in Civet's kitchen."

Monkey heaved a large sigh. "Let me help you two heroes." He reached a paw behind himself and plucked a hair from his tail. "When you tell this hair to change, it will become a chain that not even I could break—and that takes some kind of chain." He tossed it into the air and it landed on Thorn's finger, where it immediately curled up like a ring. "It should hold Civet—if you can ever get that mist stone away from her."

"I hope we'll be able to return the hair to you," I said politely—though I was sure he was going to wind up in the most dismal of the dragon dungeons.

But I don't think Monkey knew the meaning of the word *doubt*. "If you don't, I'll come looking for it." He began to wring the water from his tiger skin. "That hair is a good deal tougher than the finger it's on."

I smiled grudgingly at Monkey. "At any rate, the next time we meet, I expect a better and a drier welcome." And with a snap of my tail and a sudden flap of my wings, I went soaring skyward toward the Weeping Mountain.

CHAPTER FIFTEEN

The moon was as bright and shiny as a new silver coin when we flew over the mountains. During that time, I had been able to do some thinking. It was easy to say that I was going to use tooth and claw to fight my way to Civet, but quite another thing to do it. I didn't want to be a warrior like Monkey, who fought more with his tongue than with his mind.

I had taken a northeastern course, so that we passed over a different stretch of mountains. Ahead of us, beyond the dark huddled shapes of the mountains, the Lost Sea began to glow as a long white line on the horizon.

Suddenly I caught a glimpse of something shiny underneath me. I banked slowly to circle back and saw something glittering beneath like a glass chip.

"What is it?" Thorn asked.

"It's a pool, if I'm not mistaken. Let's have a drink before we go on."

The pool lay in a rocky hollow and hardly seemed more than four meters long and a meter at its deepest. Hundreds of tall, slender reeds, almost black in color, surrounded the northern edge of the stagnant water.

After taking a long, thirsty drink, I felt the grassy stems of some of the reeds that grew at one end of the pool. "These would make torches, I suppose. They would be good against Civet's magical cutouts." I tried to yank out some of the reeds but their stems slipped through my claws. "Bring your knife over."

Under my direction, Thorn gathered all of the reeds, splitting some of them into long slender fibers so that we could begin to tie the other reeds into bundles of twelve. Then, with a sack improvised from the boy's shirt, we flew on.

The sun was just beginning to rise as we reached

the edge of the Lost Sea; but since we were flying, we had no trouble at all during the crossing. Shortly before noontime we reached the northern edge of the sea, where the land rose in a series of ledges until it ended in a wide spacious plateau. In the very center of the plateau rose a perfect black cone of a mountain a kilometer or so high.

"That's Civet's home," I said.

I began to work my way downward until we were in the lesser currents. I banked slowly, descending in a slow spiral through the air. The mountain seemed to loom higher and higher.

Odd white lumps dotted the plateau everywhere. It wasn't until we had swept lower that we saw that they were bleached bones—spines and ribs strewn all about like broken necklaces. Here and there were large skulls as slender and pointed as arrowheads.

"What happened?" Thorn called in awe.

"Those are bones of some of the dragons who have tried to capture Civet." I landed gently. "I can't say that I like her sense of decor very much."

When the boy had slid off my neck, we stalked warily toward the gate. It had been carved from some translucent stone like jade into the likeness of a massive, gluttonous beast with a mouth big enough to swallow whole oxen. Its eyes were huge and faceted, but its cheeks seemed to be covered in feathers swelling from either side of the hungry, fanged mouth.

As we drew closer, we could see that the feathers and the lips and even the fangs had each, in turn, been carved into pouncing birds and coiled snakes, each trying to devour the other. And the facets of the eyes were really some hungry little demonic faces, each one distinct from the other. The green stone itself was shot with little red veins that made the monstrous gate seem almost like real flesh.

"It almost looks alive," Thorn murmured.

"It may very well have been once." I took out one of the torches from the bag over Thorn's shoulder. "When I was little, we used to come here for picnics. But this is one of her 'improvements.' "

Thorn lit the torch before we entered the gate. It seemed to leer as we stepped through, and a breeze suddenly slipped out as if the mountain itself were heaving a great moan—like some sleeper finally coming awake.

We followed a narrow tunnel that wound downward for about thirty meters and then suddenly spiraled sharply upward again, then twisted to the left and then corkscrewed downward once more. Tunnels led away on either side, and I began to lose track of all the twists and turns. It seemed that Civet had made a good many changes within the mountain as well.

We had almost burned through the third torch when we reached the first of the caverns. Nearly fifty meters in diameter and fifteen meters high, it was filled with stalactites hanging from the ceiling and stalagmites rising from the floor. I kicked the nearest one. "They were formed by mineral deposits as the water slowly seeped through the mountain," I explained. "There's a tale that my grandfather imprisoned his own brother somewhere inside this mountain."

"When did that happen?" Thorn poked the nearest stalagmite.

"Back when the world was young and an alliance of greedy creatures tried to claim it as their own; but they were opposed by the Five Masters—the Serpent Lady, the Archer, the Lord of the Flowers, the Unicorn and my great-grandfather." I looked around, feeling the weight of history.

"It was a desperate war, and for a time we were driven from our kingdoms into the mountain wildernesses beneath the sea. My granduncle allowed an enemy war band into the fortress itself. My great-grandfather died allowing the other Masters to escape." I touched a drop of moisture on one of the stone columns. "Later, when my grandfather led the dragons to victory, he captured his brother. One day they disappeared and my grandfather returned by himself. No one knows what happened, but he's said to have placed his brother somewhere inside this mountain. The water is supposed to be his tears."

Thorn shuddered. "I don't know about that. But the stones look like rows of teeth."

I should have made Thorn light a new torch, but I got caught up in my own memories instead. "We used to call this place the throne room," I whispered, and the words circled eerily around the walls.

Thorn held his torch near the closest wall. The stone was shaped in wide, curving surfaces like curtains, complete with folds. And as we walked toward the center of the cavern, Thorn would point to smaller sections of stone that, in his own mind, suggested banners or even tapestries blowing in the wind.

At the other end we paused by a squat, pyramid-shaped stalagmite some two meters high. Part of one side had collapsed so that it almost resembled a throne. I nodded to the strange stone formation. "My brother and I and all our cousins used to take turns sitting there." I made a face. "Of course, my brother hogged it most of the time. He said he was already king anyway."

"But did he—" Thorn's words were drowned out by a growl from the distant shadows. The torch dropped from his startled fingers. A newer torch would have continued to burn; but this one, almost completely used up already, simply sputtered and died. The cavern was plunged immediately into darkness. The growl echoed and reechoed until it sounded as if there were a hundred beasts around us.

"I'm sorry—" he began, but my groping paw found his shoulder.

It was a catastrophe, but this was no time to scold him. "Never mind. Light a new torch." While he fumbled in his sash for his flint and knife, I found the bag of torches and took out a new one. As the growling drew closer, he began frantically striking sparks with mad scratching sounds. I held the torch close to where I thought I had seen a momentary spark. He kept on stroking the flint feverishly until the torch caught fire in a sudden flash of bright, fierce light. At that very instant, we saw the huge, low-slung body of a tiger not more than five meters away.

With a gasp, Thorn dropped the flint and knife. "Steady," I snapped at him and thrust the torch into his hands. "This is our best weapon anyway." The tiger crouched, snarling as if it hated the light. It was answered by a growl behind us. I turned to see a second tiger pad between the stone columns, and then a third.

"Watch the first one," I told the boy and took another torch from his bag.

The tiger by the throne began to lash its tail, its body tensing, as I held my torch against his. It lit almost immediately.

"But why—" the boy started to ask. His eyes were on me rather than on the tiger.

It chose that very second to spring. "Watch out," I cried. The tiger's body arched through the air with its muscular front legs extended, its roar deafening our ears.

One moment the tiger loomed over us, murderous

fangs bared, its claws reached for a deadly slash. And then I had used my own torch to strike one of its legs. The next moment the tiger had disappeared. All that remained was a large piece of black paper burning in the air as it slowly fluttered to the rocky floor. There was just enough of the paper left to show the outline of a catlike tail and hindlegs.

"That's what you have to do." I faced behind us toward the two other tigers. They had just been in the act of springing when they saw me turn. They caught themselves, settling back for a moment.

"Was it real?" the boy asked.

"You would have found out quickly enough if those claws had ever struck." I watched, satisfied, as the tiger's ashes drifted overhead. "It has substance until the fire destroys its powers."

One of the tigers swung away suddenly, so that it was lost behind a row of stalagmites. Its paws struck the stones like velvet hammers.

I glanced at Thorn to make sure he was watching the front. He was turning his head slowly while he scooped up his flint and knife to tuck away in his sash. "Did you kill it?" he wondered.

"It wasn't truly alive." I swung carefully around

to face the third tiger. "Or rather it had only been given a little bit of Civet's soul. She's even weaker now for its loss." I looked all around the cavern but I couldn't see the second tiger. About ten meters away I saw the oval mouth of a tunnel. It was perhaps a meter wide but two meters high—enough to take myself and a rider. Even better, the tigers could only attack from one direction.

"I want you to climb on my back," I explained to the boy, "so that you can face behind us. I'm going to make a dash for the tunnel. And be ready to duck when I tell you."

"All right," Thorn said tensely.

I squatted down on the stones, twisting my head this way and that to watch for tigers. Even so, I couldn't look in every direction while the boy got onto my back.

"Look out," I heard the boy call and turned my head just in time to see the tiger leaping over the throne. The boy thrust his torch up stiffly, but I had the reach on him. The next moment my torch had found the creature; and it had disappeared in a quick puff of flame.

Claws suddenly raked my back. The last tiger had

taken the opportunity to strike from behind. Craning my head around me, I saw it clinging to my hindquarters, one paw stretching out to slash the boy. The boy swung his torch wildly at the tiger and just caught its paw. The tiger just had time to snarl before it changed into a bit of fiery paper.

"Well done." I blew out my own torch and triumphantly handed it back to him to stow away. "You're becoming a regular little warrior."

"That's more than I ever expected to hear from you." He sounded rather pleased, but it was quickly replaced by worry. "You're bleeding."

"The scratches look like shallow ones," I said and gave them a quick lick after he had hopped down.

"Shouldn't you do something else for those cuts?" He still sounded worried.

"The longer we delay, the more time Civet has to prepare new surprises for us." I began to limp forward grimly.

CHAPTER SIXTEEN

The tunnel eventually led to a flight of forty steps that opened into a cavern so large that we could not even see the ceiling or the far walls, only the tall rocky cones that in some places had fused into columns.

A wide canyon divided the cavern in half—with only a high stone arch linking the two sides. The arch was so thin and narrow that it seemed more like milky, orange-colored glass than stone.

Thorn tested it uncertainly with his foot. "It seems solid enough."

"It was when we used to play on it." I nudged the boy from behind. "Let's go."

Taking one cautious step at a time, he was nearly to the center of the arch when a crossbow string twanged maliciously.

"Down." With one foot I flattened him against the stone, and then I felt the sharp point of a crossbow bolt hit my left shoulder and stay there. I fell from the bridge, blinking at the pain. In knocking the boy down I had also made him lose his torch, so that it fell with me into the canyon, and a large number of unlit torches as well—I suppose they had fallen from his bag.

Painfully I spread my wings and banked, almost scraping my snout against one side of the canyon. Scrabbling, my claws found holds among the rocks and I held on for a moment, trying to get my breath back. The torch was a small bright circle of light as it tumbled lazily down into the canyon.

I was still clinging to the rocks when the boy called from above the canyon. "Shimmer, are you all right?"

I almost told the boy that I was fine; but I suddenly realized it was better for the moment if everyone thought I was dead. That way we might be able to draw the enemy out into the open, because the sniper would probably go directly after Thorn. I knew it was cruel not to answer the boy and even crueler to use him as bait; but I didn't intend to let him come to any harm. I resolutely shoved myself from the rock and began to climb upward with slow, quiet beats of my wings.

The boy called to me several times, each time his voice sounding higher and more worried. Even so, I held my tongue. The last time the boy tried to speak to me, his words broke off in a sob as if he were mourning my death. I was startled for a moment, since I don't think there was anyone else in this world who cared whether I was alive or dead. I nearly answered him right then, but I held my tongue when I heard the slow scraping noises—as if someone, most likely the boy, was crawling on his or her belly.

I decided it was probably the boy retreating back along the stone arch. Turning my face to the canyon side where we had been, I tried to hover as I probed blindly for footholds among the rocks. Then, moving as carefully as a fly, I made my way out of the canyon. I had just managed to slip in among the stalagmites when I saw the light appear on the far side of the canyon.

I wondered what a light was doing over there. Suddenly a small hand appeared, holding a lit torch. "Come and get me if you can," Thorn shouted in a voice that would have sounded more defiant if it hadn't cracked with nervousness. And he thrust the torch firmly into a crack in the side of one stalagmite.

A crossbow string twanged and a heavy bolt knocked chips from a stalagmite just to the left.

"Try again," Thorn taunted, his voice sounding firmer.

I simply closed my eyes and sighed. Instead of returning to my side of the canyon, as I had expected, Thorn had gone to the other side—I suppose with some fool notion of avenging me. I might have appreciated his show of bravery and grief if he had displayed them on the same side as myself. As it was, I would now have to reveal myself and fly across the canyon to protect him—and that meant risking another crossbow bolt.

"Come on," the boy jeered at our invisible enemy. "What are you waiting for?"

There was only the slow cranking sound of a crossbow string being drawn back. The enemy could afford to wait. Unfortunately, I couldn't—not if I wanted to save the boy.

Trying as much as possible to keep my weight off my wounded shoulder, I slipped among the stalagmites until I had the stone arch between myself and our enemy. Then, bracing my hindlegs against the base of a column, I picked out a wide space between two stalagmites on the far side. It seemed to me I could hear the sounds of boots scraping over the rocks—as if the sniper were finally closing in on Thorn.

I have definitely made better takeoffs than that particular one; but then I usually had four legs to use, not three. Recovering from my clumsy leap, I began to beat my wings rapidly, trying to keep my flight path paralleling the natural curve of the archway. Even so, I was anxiously aware of how much of me was still exposed to the sniper.

The crossbow string twanged. I resisted the urge to cringe because it would only slow me down—perhaps fatally. Instead, I dove for the far edge. The bolt ricocheted from the top of the archway, barely missing me.

I landed on my wounded shoulder and couldn't help gasping at the jagged pain that raced from my shoulder through the rest of my body. Even so, I managed to scramble to my legs and drag myself into the safety of the stone columns.

I lay there, breathing a deep sigh of relief. The crossbow string was drawn back with the slow, steady clicks of the crossbow gears. There was something deadly and ominous about the sound, as if it were some timepiece slowly counting down our last few minutes of life.

"I'm here now, boy," I whispered. "So don't worry anymore."

But there was only a grim, deadly silence.

"Thorn?" I called softly, but there was still no response.

"Speak to me, Thorn." Worried now, I didn't even bother trying to keep my voice down. My words echoed around the cavern and I waited tensely. When the boy did not answer, I began to think the worst. Had the enemy already managed to kill him? Was I too late? I desperately began to wriggle through the maze of stalagmites toward the light that marked Thorn's spot.

"Are you all right, boy?" I thrust my head urgently between two narrow stalagmites. To my surprise and confusion, I found Thorn's bag with a dozen torches— and no Thorn.

I squirmed into a small oval space surrounded by tall stone columns. I still found it hard to believe that the boy was gone. Amazed, I picked up the bag as if the boy could be hidden beneath it. Apparently Thorn had gone out hunting the sniper by himself. With a shake of my head, I laid the bag back down. I was definitely going to have to stop underestimating that boy. I found it impossible simply to sit there while the boy was doing all the fighting. Deciding to help, I stuck my head out from around the stalagmite that held the torch.

A crossbow twanged from only a few meters away. I barely ducked in time as the wicked-looking bolt embedded itself in the stone just about where my head had been. And then the next moment, I heard Thorn giving out the war cry of the Lost Sea clan— I suppose in imitation of me. It was followed by a yell of pain. Was it the sniper or Thorn?

"Thorn?" I called out in alarm. Suddenly I had this strange, helpless feeling—as if someone had ripped off my wings and pitched me back into the canyon.

"Thorn?" I said, and when there still wasn't any answer, I shouted, "THORN?" But there was only silence.

It was odd; but after my mother died, I thought I had armored myself against ever again feeling that wild sense of grief. But it was back now—a terrible aching kind of emptiness that gnawed at my insides and made everything in the world seem petty and ridiculous compared to my loss.

Of course, I hadn't let anyone get close to me since I had begun my years of wandering. But I had liked the boy's cheerfulness and his courage, which would have done credit to someone triple his size and age. Despite that affection—or because of it—I should have followed my first instincts and left him with Monkey. My own moment of weakness had now cost Thorn his life.

Something scraped on the rocks nearby. I might be too late to save the boy; but at least I could avenge him. Shouting my war cry, I sprang out from behind the stalagmites.

It was a combination of shock and my bad shoulder

that made me fall flat on my face. There, lounging against a stone column as if he owned the cavern, was Thorn. "I thought you were dead." He sounded angry and confused all at the same time.

"It was to fool the sniper." Embarrassed, I got to my feet. "Bring something for bandages, will you?"

Thorn fetched the bag of torches and emptied them on the floor. "You set me up as a target." He showed me a hurt expression.

I sat down on my haunches and yanked the torch from the stalagmite. "Before you call me any nasty names, let me point out that you turned the tables on me rather neatly." I set the torch against the bolt in my shoulder. Instantly, the bolt disappeared in a quick spurt of smoke. "After all, I became the bait instead." When the wound began to bleed, I started to lick it.

"You almost spoiled it with your talking." He began to tear the bag into strips—and looked as if he wished he was ripping up my hide instead.

I stuck the torch back into the crack. "It takes a while to perfect teamwork."

"Teamwork?" He began to knot the strips together

with short, hard jerks. "I thought you said only equals could make up a team."

I chose my compliment carefully. There was no sense swelling his head. "Yes, well, associating with me seems to have brought out some rather dragonish qualities in you." I sat back as he started to wind the bandage around the wound in my shoulder.

"I don't know if I like that idea." He tied the ends of the bandage into a knot. "In the past few days, I've heard an awful lot about a dragon's sense of honor and precious little about a dragon's sense of gratitude."

He could be as exasperating as he could be brave; and I forgot just how much I had missed him a moment ago. "There's no pleasing you, is there? Isn't it enough that a princess of—"

He gave a laugh and waved his hand airily. "I know all about your pedigree." Leaving me still spluttering in indignation, he gathered the torches in one arm. "Are we going to have enough torches?"

I got to my feet. "We'll find out soon enough, won't we?"

CHAPTER SEVENTEEN

We had to fight our way through more tunnels and
caverns, but I must say that the boy proved steady
enough—making up in courage what he lacked in
skill. Unfortunately, we ran all too quickly through
our precious store of torches. We only had two left
as we entered the largest and loveliest and most dangerous cavern of all. But if we captured Civet, we
wouldn't have to worry about traps. Anything less
that her capture would mean our own deaths. It simpli-
fied matters considerably.

The cavern was circular in shape and about three hundred and fifty meters in diameter. The walls themselves seemed covered with giant tapestries of lace that glowed a soft rosy red in the torchlight.

"What made those?" Thorn stared up at the stone lacework.

I knew the cavern well from my childhood and had asked the very same question then, so I could now give Thorn the very same explanation my own father had given me. "Long ago, some plants must have managed to grow here, or moss, or lichen." I glanced only momentarily at the lovely stone tapestries. My attention was all for the center of the cavern, where I was sure we would meet Civet. "Water seeped in and the minerals settled out to take the form of the plants until the plants were dead. Now only the shapes remain."

Thorn's eyes seemed to trace the shapes and patterns in the stony lace. "It's beautiful."

I plucked at the strap of his bag. "Come along. We're not on a pleasure tour, you know."

In the very center of the cavern, the lacy stalagmites and stalactites had fused together to form what looked like a grove of trees with intricate webs of roots and branches. Hanging from the ceiling all around the grove were stone formations that looked like chandeliers and lamps of delicate scrollwork.

We had just neared the edge of the grove when five swordswomen dropped from out of the tops of the trees. For a moment their hair flared like black flame as they fell. In each of their left hands was a huge cutlass and in each of their right hands was a whip.

Thorn thrust his torch at the women, but they only smiled. One of them flung back her right hand and then brought it forward with a sudden jerk, wrapping the thongs around the torch itself. Thorn gave a cry as the torch was torn from his grasp. Almost immediately the flames spread up the thongs to the first woman; and she vanished even as the torch itself went flying past. Her sisters, however, were now between us and the torch.

Sounding my clan's war cry, I charged them, but my shoulder slowed me down. Three of them threw back their whips and, with sharp cracks, wrapped the thongs of their whips around my left leg, below my injured shoulder. I tried to resist when they pulled, but the pain was too great. My leg went out from underneath me and I fell face forward. The last swordswoman had dropped her own whip so she could swing her cutlass up over her head in both hands.

As she stepped in, I thought it was all over for me. I was lying helpless with my chest against the rock floor and my neck stretched out conveniently for a beheading. I didn't reckon with Thorn and neither did she.

His knife went flying through the air, turning end over end. Of course, a kitchen knife isn't meant to be used quite that way, so the woman had time to duck; but it bought me the precious seconds that I needed.

I twisted my long neck around, got hold of her leg and, with a sudden jerk, flung her into the others so that the four of them fell backward in a heap onto the torch. Immediately they flared into fiery paper cutouts.

I got to my feet sullenly. "I guess I truly owe you my life this time."

He trotted over to fetch the torch. "You make it sound like a crime."

"It would be to some creatures." When the paper

warriors had burned up, the thongs about my leg had disappeared. I got up rather shakily. "I've never been too keen on the social graces—"

"Then you haven't changed any." The boy shrugged.

I swung my head around to glower at him. "Please allow me to thank you in my own way."

The boy mocked me lightly with his eyes. "Oh, is that what you're doing? I'm glad you told me, or I wouldn't have recognized it."

I wagged a claw at him. "If I had known you were going to be so obnoxious, I would never have let you save my life."

He gave me an insolent bow. "My apologies. Next time I'll let the sword cut your neck."

The whole notion was so ridiculous that I couldn't stay annoyed with him. He had a knack for poking holes through my sense of dignity. "Well"—I wrinkled my snout—"you needn't go that far."

We lit the second-to-last torch as we entered the grove of stone trees. It was slow progress trying to climb over the tree roots and ducking underneath the branches. But suddenly we found ourselves in a kind of clearing in which sat seven pools.

An outer ring was formed by six pools, each about five meters wide and two meters deep. Drops of water struck their surfaces in soft, liquid music. When Thorn held his torch near the surface of one pool, we could just make out the white and yellow crystals growing on the bottom. They grew in such tight clusters that they looked like flowers. Some had long, slender spikes and looked a little like chrysanthemums.

Thorn looked longingly at the pool. "I wish I could throw myself in there."

I felt rather hot and dusty myself. "So do I—but in a place like this, it's best to be cautious."

A larger pool sat in the center of the ring. Ten meters wide and four meters deep, the pool itself seemed completely empty of water now, but the stalagmites rising from its center were encrusted with golden flowers that glowed with a soft light of their own.

I crept warily over to a bare column of orange stone that grew on the left side of the pool. A small metal hammer hung by thongs from a projection. "Keep a sharp lookout," I warned Thorn and, getting up on my hindlegs, stretched myself over the pool's edge so I could strike the column with my good foot.

The column gave off a low ringing sound—like a bell buried far beneath the earth, but so low and deep that it was almost like a moan.

The air began to stir leisurely over the center of the pool, and a small dot of green light appeared, widening as it rippled outward to touch the very edge of the pool. I drew back quickly, waiting for Civet's next trick.

Another circle appeared and a third, and the pool was filled with a subdued, dark green light that reminded me of the shadows beneath the ancient forest giants. Far, far away I heard a soft hissing that grew steadily louder as the green light began to bubble and spin in little whirlpools and send strange shadows whirling around the stone trees.

Slowly, a small, dainty girl of about sixteen rose from out of the pool until she seemed to be standing on the surface of the green light. I blinked my eyes, a little surprised. She was wearing clothes that humans had not worn for thousands of years—though instead of plain cotton her costume had been cut of expensive silk. Over her shoulders was a short, pleated jacket with brown batik designs that reminded me of the markings on a civet cat. Her long, trailing dress matched her jacket, and I suppose that the soft hissing sound I had heard had been made by the dress hem sliding over stone. On her head, though, was a turban of costly gold cloth.

She also seemed to have emptied out a small treasure chest of gold, jade and precious stones to wear. Besides her earrings, she wore a ring on each finger and bracelets, brooches and a massive necklace. Despite all that I managed to pick out the mist stone, which hung from a slender golden chain around her neck. So I knew that this must be Civet.

I suppose she had meant to impress us, but her entire outfit only struck me as being a bit flashy and overdressed—like that of a child who has borrowed her mother's best clothes so she can play at being a hostess.

She only added to that impression when she actually spoke, because her voice was childishly high—no matter how haughty she tried to sound. "Who dares to summon me?" she demanded.

I crouched, ready to fight my way through hordes of monsters and warriors. "You've much to answer for."

"And so have you." One hand gripped the side

of her dress as she whisked the hem elegantly over the surface of the pool. "By the power of water and earth, take them."

Immediately the water in the three farther pools pushed upward like living worms that arched over Civet's head to cascade down upon both of us. I was knocked over by the sudden force of the flood and washed backward until I came up hard against the grove of stone trees. Stunned, I lay gasping among their roots.

Lithe as a cat, Civet strode to the very edge of the pool and leaped down. At her word of command, the roots of the nearby trees suddenly slipped out of the rocky floor and rose like gritty tentacles to wrap themselves around my legs and body. One even caught me across the mouth like a gag. I shut my eyes, straining every muscle as I pulled and wiggled, but even my immense strength could not break their stony grip. To my right I could hear Thorn grunting as if he, too, were trying to break free.

Then I thought of shrinking myself or changing into some more slippery shape, like that of a snake. Desperately I sketched a magical symbol in the air with my claw; but without a spoken spell to power the sign, my claws were simply scratching the air.

Civet's dress hissed with silken softness over the stone floor as she strode right up to me. "It's no use struggling, you know. I've got you." She spoke with all the smugness of a child who had just bested another in some wrestling match.

I slumped bitterly. I had failed, like all the other dragons. Eventually, I supposed, my bones would be tossed outside to be added to the remains of all the other failures.

"I'm sorry that I had to do this, but only one of us can survive." She tested my bonds. "I do hope you're going to be a good sport about the whole thing."

My only answer was to squirm against the stone roots, but I merely succeeded in rubbing my hide raw in several places.

"You see, it's useless." She patted the root that bound my chest. "So why don't you give me your word of honor not to use your magic. Then I could remove your gag and give you a last meal and have a little chat before I . . . ah . . . well, do away with you." She smiled at me awkwardly.

Unfortunately, she hadn't gagged Thorn. "And

who's going to cook your meals?" he asked.

Civet started to motion behind her. "Why, my servants . . ." She rubbed her forehead in annoyance. "Oh, bother, you've disposed of all of my servants." For once she didn't seem to know what to do—like an actress who finds she's using the wrong script. Her puzzlement and frustration were plain in her voice when she spoke again. "And it's going to be quite a while before I'll have the energy to make more. Making the water and stalagmites move has tired me out."

"How would you like a real flesh-and-blood servant?" Thorn sounded anxious and excited. "One who didn't have to be afraid of a cooking fire?"

I twisted, but the gag held my head rigid so I couldn't see the boy. Well, I thought to myself bitterly, so much for the promise he had made when he had first asked to go with me. At that time, he had said that he would never let me down; and during our long journey, I had actually begun to have faith in him. But now I knew he was just as treacherous and deceitful as the rest of his kind.

Civet cupped her chin in one hand. "Hmm, I do have a rather high casualty rate with my cooks. One step too close to the fire, and poof"—she flung out her hand to accent the word—"they go up in smoke."

"And paper servants can't be much company for a clever person like you," Thorn coaxed.

"No, they aren't very good conversationalists," she said with a sad little laugh. "No matter what spells I use, I can't make them think."

Thorn's voice was warm and friendly. "How can you celebrate your victory when you have to cook your own meal?"

Civet seemed amused as she pushed a strand of hair underneath her turban. "And I suppose you want to help me, is that it?"

Thorn's voice took on an almost professional assurance—as if he were mimicking Knobby, his old employer. "People were giving parties all the time at the inn where I worked. I know what to do."

I struggled to tell her that the boy was probably lying, but the only sounds I could make around the gag were angry snarls. Civet nodded to me. "Your former employer doesn't seem to like the idea."

"I wasn't about to use her as a reference anyway," Thorn said.

Civet bit her lip thoughtfully. "Well, it really *has*

been a long time since I've had any real company."
She smiled almost shyly. "Perhaps I'll give you a try."
She swept her hand through the air as she murmured
something. A moment later I heard a harsh, grating
sound—as if the tree roots were sliding back.

Thorn appeared almost immediately in my line of
sight. He moved slowly as he tried to rub the circula-
tion back into his arms. "Now, which way is it to
the kitchen?" he asked eagerly.

"It's back there." She pointed beyond the pools
toward the shadows at the rear of the cavern and
then swung her arm around so she could wag her
index finger at him—almost like a stern, older sister.
"But just remember one thing. I'm only going to
give you this one chance. Give me any reason to doubt
you and you'll be sorry."

The boy swallowed. "I've seen what you've done
to your enemies." He turned and started for the
kitchen. As he shuffled past, I tried to trip him with
the tip of my tail, but I could not even move that.

"Traitor," I shouted, but, much to my frustration,
the sound only came out as a growl because of the
stone root gagging my mouth.

Thorn gave a little jump. He stared at me as if

hurt, and then he shrugged his shoulders in a great show of carelessness. "I want to live."

I squirmed against the dense tangle of roots. "I trusted you," I said, but again the sound was muffled by the gag.

He spread out his hands. "I can give a good guess as to what you're saying. Try to look at things from my point of view. What's honor and good faith to a skeleton?" But while his back was to Civet, he managed to wink at me. Then he slipped quickly out of sight.

Had I underestimated the boy once again? And yet what could he hope to do against anyone so powerful as Civet? I could only lie there helplessly, waiting to find out.

CHAPTER EIGHTEEN

I still hadn't figured out what he was up to when he returned with a large green bowl. Civet was sitting on a stumplike rock beside me. For the tenth time or so, she asked me to give her my oath not to use magic. "We could have a very nice chat while we eat," she suggested wistfully. "I really would like to talk to someone who remembers the old days."

I simply glared at her as I had the other times.

"Well, perhaps you'll change your mind," she

sighed, and held out her hands for the bowl. Long streamers of steam rose from its mouth.

"It's hot," Thorn warned her as he handed her the bowl.

Civet balanced it carefully between her fingertips. "Noodles?" she asked unhappily. "Is that all?"

"I thought you wanted a quick meal." Thorn smiled ingratiatingly.

Exasperated, Civet set the bowl down on her lap. "I thought you knew a lot of elegant party dishes."

Thorn slapped a hand to his forehead. "Did I make you think that?" He spread out his hands apologetically. "We did have a lot of parties at the inn, but they were always for simple farmers."

Civet pressed her lips together tightly as if she were trying to decide if Thorn was making fun of her. I think she was really much less confident and secure than she pretended to be. "I've a good mind to turn you into a cockroach and stamp on you."

Thorn dropped his head like a good servant. "And who'd wash the dishes?"

"Who indeed?" Civet wondered in a dry voice. She picked up the ivory chopsticks that had been laid across the mouth of the bowl. "In any case, the joke is on you, because I had intended to give you the first taste."

Even in the dim light, I could see how Thorn paled. Had he put some kind of poison in it? I began to regret some of the harsh things I had thought about him.

"I . . . unh . . . nibbled in the kitchen," he mumbled.

Civet smiled as if he had just confirmed her suspicions. "Really?" She stirred her chopsticks around inside the bowl. "They say that poison discolors ivory." She held the chopsticks up to study the tips and seemed mildly surprised that they were the same color as before. "Still, there are so many sophisticated poisons nowadays."

"But I wouldn't use a poison," Thorn insisted—rather guiltily I thought. "You can trust me."

Civet raised her eyebrows in a superior fashion. "I haven't trusted anyone since my own dear, loving father sent me to my death."

"He what?" Thorn's eyes widened in horror.

"The King Within the River had seen me on the riverbank and wanted me for his bride." With an abrupt swoop of her hand, Civet dipped her chopsticks back into the bowl. "And my father was too scared to refuse."

"And who was the King?" Thorn asked.

"He was a magical creature who once ruled all of the Arrow River." She regarded Thorn with frosty contempt. "The waters didn't rise or fall a millimeter without his permission, and all the boats and river villages had to pay tribute to him—including my village, which became River Glen."

Such things used to happen thousands of years ago when the humans still lived in weak, isolated tribes. Disorganized, they had been easy victims for certain powerful magical creatures who might call themselves kings and queens but who were little more than bandits at heart. At least her story matched her ancient costume.

"I think I would have run away," Thorn said. He seemed fascinated by the long, trailing noodles lifted from the bowl.

"So would most people." Civet dumped the noodles back into the bowl. "And I was tempted to hide. Who would want to go live in that muddy old river when they could live in my valley?" Her face grew suddenly peaceful. "There was never a valley quite as lovely as mine."

Seized by some strange impulse, she turned to me. "Do you remember how the pine trees filled almost the whole valley?" she asked eagerly. "I spent as much time as I could in the cool, fragrant shadows." She lifted her arms in a slowly rising angle, as if she could trace the sweep of the forest top. "And do you remember how the trees used to go right up the sides of the mountains?"

At that moment she seemed more like some homesick child than a wicked sorceress. I had gotten so used to thinking of her as a hateful creature that it was hard to believe she was capable of loving anything. But in her own way, I suppose, she had loved the forest as much as I had loved my sea, or she wouldn't have gone to the King Within the River.

Perhaps she had been telling the truth when she had said that she wanted to reminisce with me about the old days. Unfortunately for her, I wasn't quite that old. We had been trading with the humans for some hundred and fifty years by the time I had been taken to the city as a fifty-year-old infant. Even so, some of the forest had been left and I remembered how the green shadows beneath the trees had reminded me very much of my own home. However, because of my bonds, all I could manage to do right then was nod my head ever so slightly.

Civet's hand dropped abruptly to her lap, as if she was disappointed by my inability to respond. She turned again to Thorn, finding him to be a better audience. "At any rate," she said with great dignity, "I couldn't let the King destroy my valley."

"That was a brave thing to do." Thorn shook his head as if in admiration.

"So everyone said." She smoothed her dress over her knee. "They tried to make it up to me by fussing over the 'wedding,' as they called it. I was given the best cloth for my wedding robe and the most precious stones, and they held a big feast on the riverbank. And my father and all the elders made speeches about what a noble sacrifice I was making and how generations to come would remember what I had done for my people. And they all wept and promised."

Her face had grown very still and her eyes took on a distant look, as if she were seeing the scene once again. "And then almost everyone crowded into the boats and escorted me out to the middle of the river.

"The people had to paddle hard just to keep the boats steady in the currents." Her lips moved mechanically as if controlled by someone else. "One by one the items of my dowry were pitched overboard." Her own head moved from side to side slowly as if she were watching. "And then there was only me.

"Father held out his hand." She raised her own hand to illustrate. "And he said, 'It's time to go.'

"And I looked beyond him for one last look at my beloved valley. The green tops of the trees looked so soft and comfortable in the warm, misty air.

" 'The King must be waiting,' Father reminded me. I turned. His eyes pleaded with me silently not to make a scene but to go willingly. Even now, he was afraid of angering the King.

"I looked at my father contemptuously. I was willing to give up my life and he would still begrudge me these few moments. I stood up carefully then so that I didn't rock the boat. Over the side I saw my face reflected on the surface of the water—a distorted reflection upset by all the ripples from the paddles.

And then I jumped and I was breaking through the surface.

"I struggled to swim as I had once swum so easily before, but my wedding robe became soaked with water quickly and felt as heavy as if it had been cut from stone. And all of my jewelry weighed like boulders." Her arms paddled furiously for a moment in the air. "I tried everything. I even wriggled like an eel, but it was no use. I felt myself falling down, down into the depths.

"It was so muddy that it was hard to see, but I was looking for the King. If anyone had ever seen him, that person had never lived to tell about it. To me he was just this big voice booming from the water when he wanted something.

"And then I thought I could just make out a shape. At first I thought it was a mask because it was so ugly. But then I realized it was a real face with a long, waving beard like pondweed. His shoulders were covered with scaled armor and his legs were squat and bent like a frog's. Slowly he raised his arms in welcome."

She looked downward, her eyes widening slowly, her mouth opening in horror and revulsion. Her reactions were so real that I almost felt as if I, too, could see the shadowy King Within the River. She seemed to be not simply remembering the scene but actually going through her death all over again. I couldn't help shivering.

Civet tilted back her head desperately, but her words came out only as a whisper, as if she were simply voicing her thoughts. "Help me. Father. Mother. Someone. Please help me." Her body twitched and one leg angled out. "He's got hold of my ankle." She wriggled and squirmed as if panicked. "He's pulling me down." Her face grew a little harsher, as if anger were replacing her fear. "He's so ugly. So terrible. How could you send me to him without asking what he looks like? It's not right. It's not right at all.

"I need air. I need light." Suddenly she gave a gasp. "The water's cold. So cold inside my lungs. I can't breathe." She made a choking sound and stiffened.

Thorn tiptoed close to her.

Her eyes blinked once. They they blinked again. She relaxed a bit, staring at Thorn with sudden recognition. "Step back," she warned him.

Thorn obeyed hastily. "I was just trying to see if you were all right. You looked like you were dying."

Civet's breath came in short, sharp hisses, as if she were still fighting to regain her breath. "The King preserved my body exactly as it was at the moment of drowning." Her shoulders rose and fell more slowly as her lungs recovered. "This is my true shape."

"And everything else has stayed fresh in your mind—like dying?"

"Yes." She touched a hand to the mist stone to reassure herself that Thorn hadn't stolen it. "That's the unfortunate drawback to that particular spell." She gestured toward her heart. "Even now I can feel the hatred welling up inside me, hot and scalding."

"I don't blame you." He made a sympathetic face. "The King sounds terrible."

"It's not just the King." She closed her eyes as her breathing grew even. "It's also the fault of my father and my tribe. They didn't even try to argue with the King or do anything." Her eyelids slid back up. "But our noodles are getting cold." Her chopsticks raised a portion of noodles again. "You really must eat your share now."

CHAPTER NINETEEN

Thorn had this strange, panicked expression on his face—like some little beast, newly trapped. "I really couldn't eat in front of the dragon."

"And I'm afraid that I must insist." Civet narrowed her eyes dangerously.

Reluctantly, as if his jaws swung on rusty hinges, Thorn opened his mouth and bent over slightly. With a little flip of her wrist, Civet thrust the noodles into Thorn's mouth.

Thorn straightened up with a stricken look, his face

going through the oddest sort of contortions. First one cheek would bulge; and then it would flatten while the other cheek bulged—as if his tongue were searching for something.

"Aren't you going to swallow?" Civet asked with mock pleasantness.

The boy choked down the entire mouthful. "I've always been taught to eat slowly."

"Maybe you'll even learn how to chew sometime." She took a handkerchief from her sleeve and wiped her chopsticks as she watched Thorn with a detached air—as if waiting for him to fall down and froth at the mouth. When she had returned the handkerchief back to her sleeve, she looked at him solicitously. "And how do you feel now?"

"Pretty good," Thorn assured her.

"Marvelous." She smiled sarcastically. "Let me know the moment you feel any signs of distress, will you?" She sounded as if she were sure there would be some. Meanwhile, in order to pass the time, she began to tell us of her life with the King Within the River.

She didn't remember the actual moment that she "changed"—as she called it. She had passed out after the water had invaded her lungs. The next thing she knew, she had woken up in a large muddy cave that the King had called his throne room, though it was more like a junk room with benches and lamps and other furnishings looted from shipwrecks and flooded villages.

The palace itself was little more than muddy caves and tunnels dug into the west bank of the Arrow River, twenty meters beneath its surface. Once inside her husband's home, she had never been allowed outside or to have contact with anyone except the paper servants, who were voiceless and almost mindless.

When the King was busy experimenting with his magic, she used to sit beside the bars of the palace gates and listen to the river as it roared by outside. Because the river was so muddy, it was impossible to see even the noonday sun, let alone any boats. But still she would dream of the day when she would return to her valley home.

However, one morning the King discovered her at the gates and beat her unmercifully, saying that she was his wife now and should learn to enjoy her new home. It was then that she realized she would never be free until she did away with him. So she pretended to have a change of heart, following him about the palace like a faithful dog.

Her husband was pleased with her meek behavior and raised no objection. And so she listened and she watched and she learned. And then, when she knew all the magic she needed to, she changed him into stone so that, as she said, the rest of his body could be as hard as his heart. And she buried him deep within the mud of his river.

Civet interrupted herself to click her chopsticks at Thorn. "How are you now? Any nausea? Heart beating faster?"

"I'm fine"—Thorn shrugged—"but your meal's gotten cold."

Civet seemed rather surprised. "It's better to be safe than sorry." She picked up a solitary noodle with her chopsticks and began to nibble it experimentally— pausing after each tiny bite to see what would happen. I glanced at Thorn. His face was screwed up expectantly. I held my breath. I was sure now that he was up to something—though I still didn't know what.

Civet lowered her chopsticks when she was fin- ished—waiting, I suppose, for some kind of reaction. She was so cautious that I could see how she had managed to last so long as she had. In the meantime, she went on with her story. "And then I was free. After almost a thousand years I was free."

Thorn seemed to think it was important to distract her by keeping her talking. "So you went home?"

She laughed sadly and shrugged. "There wasn't any home to go back to." She made a paddling motion with one hand. "When I swam back, I found all the old mat huts had been replaced by buildings of pink stone, and the long pilings of the wharves had sunk into the riverbank like fangs. I could hardly even see the sunlight because of all the horrid chemicals and filth in the water."

Thorn wrinkled his eyebrows as if puzzled. "What happened?"

"Time." She shook her head ruefully. "I'd forgotten that it had taken me a thousand years to learn the spells I needed." She crossed her legs abruptly. "But though the clothes and the language of the people had changed, I recognized their faces." Her voice was suddenly cold and hard and bitter. "The seed of my tribe was still there, scattered throughout the city. And I knew I could never rest until that treacherous seed was swept away."

"But why?" Thorn blurted out in protest. "They weren't the ones who sent you to the King."

"I sacrificed everything for them, and they destroyed my lovely forest anyway." She looked at her own stone trees as if they were a poor substitute. "They betrayed my trust. And they betrayed the land. They had cut down all the trees of the forest, so that the mountains were worn and gullied and what few fields remained were being killed by all the waste from the mines and the factories." Civet clenched her fist and the light in the central pool shimmered, sending reflections of green light shining all around the cavern like a living net.

Thorn kept his eyes on her as she used her chopsticks to lift up a bunch of noodles. "Well, why didn't you send the river against them?"

"It wasn't strong enough." She held the noodles just before her mouth. "The buildings were made of stone and they were two or more stories high." She shoved the noodles into her mouth, chewing and swallowing absently as she recounted her triumph. "What I needed was an entire ocean. I explored the area and discovered that it was the trade with the dragons that had made my little village grow into that ugly city." She adjusted her grip on her chopsticks. "And since the dragons of the Inland Sea were to blame, I decided to take their ocean."

Thorn shifted uneasily from one leg to another as if no longer sure what to do. "But why didn't you use it right away?"

She thrust her head indignantly toward Thorn. "Because I decided that they didn't deserve a quick end." Pressing her lips together, she gave a firm little nod. "I wanted them to suffer as the land had suffered."

And, I couldn't help thinking, as she had suffered too.

Between mouthfuls of noodles, Civet spoke with all the prim self-justification of an older sister disciplining a mob of unruly younger brothers and sisters. However, her punishments hadn't been with strokes of a bamboo rod. Instead, she had used floods each generation—floods just large enough to destroy some of the crops and factories and homes but not enough to drive the people away.

Civet might have gone on working her mischief indefinitely if Monkey hadn't arrived to spoil everything.

"I waited almost too long to destroy the city." She

shook her head ruefully—as if at her own stupidity. "Oh, I knew I could flood the city all right, but I wasn't sure I could get away from Monkey afterward." She cupped the mist stone upon her palm. "And I had to be free to hunt down anyone who escaped from the city." Her hand closed around the stone. "My revenge had to be a complete and thorough one."

Thorn's nose twitched as if he were tempted to tell her that she had failed to kill anyone, but he controlled himself. She would probably find out soon enough once she went out hunting again.

"And then I remembered the Keeper's mist stone. With it, I knew I could escape from Monkey." She let go of the milky stone around her neck. "It was risky going after it, but it was worth all the trouble." She lifted another bunch of noodles from the bowl. "As soon as I've had a proper rest, I'll start to search for the survivors." Suddenly she drew her eyebrows together. "You dirty little pig," she blurted out angrily. "You lost one of your hairs in the noodles."

I remembered that hair that Monkey had given Thorn. I tried to look at Thorn's finger, but the angle was wrong.

In the meantime, Civet had dropped her chopsticks and raised a hand as if she were going to pluck something out of her mouth. I suppose that this was the moment for which Thorn had been waiting so impatiently.

The word seemed to explode from his lips. "CHANGE!" he shouted.

CHAPTER TWENTY

Civet's eyes widened in surprise. The bowl fell from her lap and shattered on the stone floor. Alarmed, she lurched to her feet just as links of chain suddenly spilled from between her lips. Her hands frantically tugged at the end of the chain, yet though the links were each as small as a thumbnail, they seemed stronger than any steel. Monkey might be a fool in other things, but he certainly knew his magic.

Civet stopped pulling almost the instant she began—hunching her shoulders instead and wincing as if in great pain. Her stomach started to swell outward, taking on a bloated look; and she lowered her hands to it. I suppose the chain links had slipped down her throat and into her belly now.

Civet's outline began to dissolve as if she were trying to change herself into a mist, but suddenly she grew solid again. A second time her outline wavered and then solidified. I guess she was in such pain that she could not concentrate long enough to say the transformation spell, or perhaps she simply could not speak clearly enough. Or maybe she didn't even have enough energy yet to work magic.

I tried to tell Thorn to get the mist stone while she was still distracted, but I could only make muffled sounds. Even so, Thorn figured out what to do. He stepped right up to her and lifted his hand.

Civet tried to shove him away, but Thorn managed to slip his hand between her arms and close his fingers around the stone. Desperately, Civet grasped his wrist and the two of them struggled for a moment. They might have still been wrestling if Thorn hadn't used his free hand to hit her in the stomach.

Civet instantly doubled up with a deep groan and she dropped her hands away from Thorn's arm. "I'm sorry," Thorn said to her, "but I can't let innocent people die."

The stone's thin gold chain broke on the first yank. All the fight seemed to go out of Civet then. Her shoulders slumped and she fell to the floor as the light within the central pool began to flicker crazily.

I growled and grumbled urgently to the boy, so that he turned his attention to me instead. "Maybe if I can free your mouth," he said, "you can change your shape or something."

He disappeared, reappearing a moment later with a heavy kitchen cleaver. "I think this might do it."

I wriggled my eyebrows in urgent agreement—and then closed my eyes while he started to whack away at the stone root, since one slip would have sent the blade slicing across my face. It took a while, but eventually I mumbled to the boy to stop and he did—more from my tone than my actual words. Then, gripping the root between my teeth, I began to twist my head from side to side. The root was still too strong, so I grunted to Thorn to begin chopping again. It took three more tries before he had weakened the root enough for me to break it.

Spitting out bits of stone, I made the sign and spoke

the spell that would shrink me to the size of a garden snake so that I could easily creep away from the loops and coils of the roots. Then I changed myself back to my usual length.

"Won't you please put her out of her misery?" Thorn nodded to Civet.

I handed the stone and its chain to Thorn and limped toward Civet as she lay on the cavern floor. When she saw me coming, she raised an arm to cover her eyes as if she did not want to see what was going to happen. Slowly I raised my foot for the killing blow.

But she was lying curled up on her side—like some poor child with a terrible stomachache. "I can't do it." I dropped my foot, angry and frustrated at my own weakness. It had been different when she had been a faceless enemy whom I knew only by her hateful reputation; but as she had talked to us, I had come to understand a few things about her.

She might have lived a good number of years and picked up a good deal of magic, but inside she hadn't grown up at all. As she had said, when her husband had preserved her body, he had also frozen her emotions. The anger and fear were still as fresh and young as her body on that day long ago. Even with the King gone, the hatred was still there poisoning her heart. It had simply found a new target in the city and, unfortunately, my own clan.

I tried to dredge up all that old harsh, bitter anger I had felt when she had been only a faceless enemy. But I knew what it was like to long for a home and then find it gone. I reminded myself that she was to blame for the loss of my sea. But I couldn't shake the feeling that she had been driven by the same sense of loss that I myself had felt. Unfortunately for everyone concerned, she could not live with her disappointments but had needed to hurt others.

"Listen to me," I said softly. "I'll spare you if you'll restore the sea."

Civet's arm slid back to the floor. Her eyes blinked open so I could see how her surprise mixed now with her pain. "Can't," she mumbled with great difficulty. "The spells . . . only work . . . once."

I sighed. It had all been so useless. My anger was almost completely gone by now, leaving only a deep, aching emptiness within me.

"Hurts," she pleaded. "Please . . . take chain . . . away."

Thorn tried shouting "Change" again, but whatever magic Monkey had put into the hair had been used up. So I tried to run through various spells, but none of them worked. Finally, I had to confess, "I don't know how. I'd have to find Monkey or some great magician." Impulsively, I rested my paw upon her forehead. "But I can do this for you." And I rapped her sharply on the temple.

Civet rolled her head slightly as she became unconscious.

Wearily—as if the entire mountain had just been laid across my shoulders—I let my foot drop to the floor. "Now what are we going to do with her?"

Thorn knelt down beside her. "Well, you can't leave her like this forever."

I plucked at my lower lip as I considered the possibilities, and then lowered my foot as an idea suddenly came to me. "I said I would need either Monkey or some powerful magician. And we can find them both in the dragon kingdoms. Maybe we could strike some kind of a bargain with her. The chain would be removed in exchange for any help she can give in restoring the sea. After all, she might be able to provide information that would help the dragon sages create new spells."

"But you can't go into the dragon kingdoms. You're an outlaw." Thorn used the broken gold chain to tie the mist stone around the ankle of my good foreleg.

I raised my foreleg to admire the mist stone. It was a pretty enough little bauble. "I think they'd give me a safe conduct long enough to announce the news to the High King of the Dragons."

Thorn got to his feet excitedly. "Maybe they'd even cancel that decree that made you an outlaw."

I found the boy's enthusiasm was infectious. "At any rate"—I smiled—"you ought to visit the coral palaces and gardens."

Thorn flattened his palm against his chest. "You're going to take me with you?"

"We've gone this far together. Why not go on a little farther?" When he still hesitated, I pretended to glower at him—though I was really beginning to feel a little anxious inside. "Don't tell me you want to quit just when I'm getting used to having you around?"

"Not exactly." He sat back on his heels. "It's just

that you were awfully quick to condemn me a little while ago."

I suppose the boy did have a point. "Harumph." I shuffled my paws uncomfortably. "Well, perhaps I should have known you wouldn't desert me so easily."

"Yes, you should have." The boy nodded.

"An-n-n-d I guess I owe you an apology." I looked at the boy in the hope that he would let me off the hook, but apparently he wasn't about to.

"Yes, you do." He folded his arms expectantly.

It was really too much for a poor dragon's soul to bear. Suddenly, as if making a last stand, I planted my feet and thrust my head forward. "But I'm not. You want too much from me. I've survived all these years because I didn't trust anyone. So you can't expect me to change my habits overnight."

"Well, I'd hate it if you strained yourself." One corner of his mouth curled up ironically.

"That's the closest I've come to apologizing in centuries." I raised my right foot truthfully.

"I can believe that." He studied me for a moment and then said cautiously, "All right. Supposing I did go with you. What would happen once we reached the ocean? Wouldn't the other dragons object to your traveling with a human?"

"They won't say anything if I'm within hitting distance of them," I promised. I suppose I owed him that much for doubting him. However, I was startled when the boy slapped his knees and began to laugh. "What's so funny?" I demanded.

His laugh subsided as he wiped a tear from his eye. "You have such a fine way of winning friends."

I cleared my throat noisily. "Well, we're family in a strange sort of way. I mean, heaven knows where my clan is because they're scattered all around the world, and you're an orphan." I shrugged. "And we already seem to have adopted one another."

The boy cocked his head to the side as if he didn't quite trust his ears. "Are you serious?"

"As serious as I'll ever be." I lowered my belly to the floor.

But the boy still didn't quite believe me. "Are you sure you want to adopt me?"

"Yes," I assured him, "though I must be mad or a glutton for punishment."

"I suppose I am too," he admitted, "so I guess we're related after all." He started to raise his hand to pat my head affectionately but then hesitated.

I wasn't a pet dog, but I had just gotten finished saying he was family. So I compromised by lowering my head and brushing my cheek lightly against his open palm. "Hurry up then. The sooner we load Civet on my back and get some food from her kitchen, the sooner we can leave."

When we were ready, I raised my head and uncovered the dream pearl so that a cool, silvery light suddenly blazed all around us. And as we passed through the mountain, its magical light went before us, making the stones of the caverns and tunnels look softer, almost like flesh. And our shadows, moving on long, stiltlike legs behind us, seemed to take on a life of their own—sometimes dodging around behind the stone columns as if playing hide-and-seek, sometimes trying to dart ahead of us.

"I think the pearl is rather hungry to show what it can do," I murmured.

Whether we had destroyed all of Civet's creatures or they had vanished once she could no longer control them with her conscious will—or perhaps because they were frightened—we met with no ambushes on the long way back.

The sun was shining when we reached the strange

carved entrance to the mountain. Even so, the magic of the pearl reached out almost invisibly. A few meters to our left the bones of a dragon skeleton seemed to stir like large, white-throated snakes.

I covered the pearl and then shaded my eyes against the light reflecting from the seafloor. "One day I'll have a home again."

"Even if we have to bring it in a drop at a time," the boy solemnly vowed.

And at that moment a great wind darted down from the skies across the plateau to swirl about the mountain opening. The wind seemed to roar to me that it would carry me around and around the world forever if I asked it. It was a dragon wind, a royal wind—one that was fit to take us to our fate.

"Yes, we're ready," I whispered. And for a moment I forgot the pain in my shoulder. And the wind coiled like a serpent around us and suddenly we were lifted skyward as easily as if we had shed all our cares and worries for the moment—as if we had cast away even our bodies and were mere ribbons of light floating in the air.

Ahead of us lay the mighty undersea kingdoms of the dragons. Eagerly I began to beat my wings.

AFTERWORD

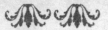

It was my original intention to retell the adventures of the Old Mother of the Waters, who destroyed an entire city in China and was able to elude capture until she swallowed a chain disguised as a strand of vermicelli. However, stories—like people—develop and grow, so only a few images have survived from the first version of this novel. And, in general, while I have tried to stay true to the spirit of the other Chinese myths that form the background of the novel, I have not tried to keep to their exact details.